P9-EAJ-721

Part One

Four Years Later

Prologue

Josie, Age 9

Beach—Whalehead, New Jersey

The Minotaur Coaster was a new addition to my favorite place on earth: Murphy's Pier in Whalehead, New Jersey.

Every summer I found this place exactly the way it was when I left: the ocean, the boardwalk, and my and Stella's special secret hiding place *under* the boardwalk.

But what I liked most of all was being with my sister, Stella. Well, she's technically my half sister, and she's my best friend. Since we live so far apart, and I can only see her during the summers, we spend every waking minute of the summer together.

We sat on the sandbar, our legs floating in the salt water. From out there, I could either face the New Jersey coastline, the boardwalk, and all of its wild excitement, or I could look out at the vast ocean and imagine that this water touched the coastline of my home, Australia.

A speedboat zoomed by, towing tandem parasailers in flight, a flock of white seabirds behind them. The parasailers waved down to me and Stella while we stacked fistfuls of wet sand on each other's shoulders.

"Ready for the fun house?" I asked her.

Stella yelled to Dad, who sat at the water's edge under a beach umbrella. "Dad, can we go to the fun house?"

He hollered back, "As long as you get yourselves water ice, too."

We trudged our way back to the beach.

Dad pulled out money, then turned his chair to face the boardwalk. "I'll watch you from here."

"Want one?"

"Nah." He patted his round belly. "I'll just have some of yours." He gave us each a hug and kissed the tops of our heads.

Stella broke away first and dashed toward the boardwalk. When she was a safe distance, she turned, giggled, and said in her New York accent, "What are you tawkin' about? I'm not sharing!"

Dad chased her. "Oh yes you are." When he caught her, they both toppled into the sand, laughing.

I pounced onto his back. "Let my sista go!" My accent was so different from Stella's, but we understood each other perfectly.

"You win. You win," Dad said. "But, for the record two against one isn't fair."

We hopped on the hot sand until we got to the boardwalk. We waved to our shore friend, Dario, who bobbed up and down on a big horse on the merry-go-round. After waiting for the oncoming traffic of surf bikes to pass, we finally got into the fun house line.

"Do you have it?" I asked Stella.

She held up the plastic tail from our kite. It had broken off last night, and I wanted to save it to remember what a great night it was. We had a special secret place where we stashed these kinds of treasures.

We entered Kevin's Fun House, zipped to the bright, shiny hall of mirrors, and paused to laugh at our ultrashort, ultratall, or ultraround selves. Then we giggled our way through foam pillars—a tight fit—and scaled the rope bridge, finally racing to the barrel that marked the loose floorboards. We waited for a crowd of toddlers to pass, and I quickly slid the barrel aside; Stella stomped on the end of the loose boards, popping them up to create enough room for us to jump to the sand below. I pulled the rope we'd tied to the underside of the boards, and the trapdoor slammed shut above us.

This was our hiding place under the boardwalk. I walked to our rock that marked the spot where we'd buried a box—not just any box. It held our special treasures. I dug it up, opened it, and added the kite tail to the gum wrapper, shell, Matchbox car, marble, Barbie, midway game tickets, and other items that represented our many summer adventures—mine and Stella's.

A few minutes later we were plopped on the edge of the boardwalk, Water Ice World paper cones in our hands, watching the bustle of vacationers who smelled like coconut sunscreen and sweat. Our feet swung over the sand below, and even though we licked, dripped water ice went onto our chins and arms.

I asked, "Stella?"

"Yeah? What?" Stella wiped red water-ice juice off her face with her sleeve.

"I love it here," I said.

"Me too."

"Can we do this forever? Exactly this same exact thing every single summer? Just like this. It's perfect, and I don't want it to ever change."

"Sure, Josie. Nothing's gonna change."

But, like all perfect things, it did.

For Joan Callaghan,
whose family beach vacations
shaped a generation

This book is a work of fiction. Any references to historical events, real people, or real places are used fictitiously. Other names, characters, places, and events are products of the author's imagination, and any resemblance to actual events or places or persons, living or dead, is entirely coincidental.

An imprint of Simon & Schuster Children's Publishing Division
1230 Avenue of the Americas, New York, New York 10020
First Aladdin hardcover edition April 2020

Jacket designed by Tiara Iandiorio
Interior designed by Mike Rosamilia
The text of this book was set in Adobe Jenson Pro.
Manufactured in the United States of America 0320 FFG
2 4 6 8 10 9 7 5 3 1
Library of Congress Cataloging-in-Publication Data
Names: Callaghan, Cindy, author. | Title: Saltwater secrets / by Cindy Callaghan. | Description: First Aladdin hardcover edition. | New York : Aladdin, 2020. | Summary: Half-sisters Stella and Josie love spending summers together at the beach, but things are harder this year, especially when new business owners exploit the natural habitat, endangering marine life and people as well.
Identifiers: LCCN 2019016959 (print) | LCCN 2019019368 (eBook) |
ISBN 9781534417458 (eBook) | ISBN 9781534417441 (hc)
Subjects: | CYAC: Sisters—Fiction. | Beaches—Fiction. | Environmental protection—Fiction. | BISAC: JUVENILE FICTION / Nature & the Natural World / Environment. | JUVENILE FICTION / Family / Siblings. | JUVENILE FICTION / Girls & Women.
Classification: LCC PZ7.C12926 (eBook) | LCC PZ7.C12926 Sal 2020 (print) | DDC [Fic]—dc23
LC record available at https://lccn.loc.gov/2019016959

Saltwater Secrets

CINDY CALLAGHAN

Aladdin
New York London Toronto Sydney New Delhi

Praise for *Saltwater Secrets*

"*Saltwater Secrets* is a whirlwind of mystery, friendship, and heart. It's the perfect summer read that will leave readers feeling empowered!"

—OLIVIA SANABIA, actress and singer (*Just Add Magic* and *Coop & Cami Ask the World*)

"Cindy Callaghan effortlessly captures the perfect teenage summer in *Saltwater Secrets*."

—ABBY DONNELLY, actress (*Just Add Magic* and *Malibu Rescue*)

"I absolutely loved this book. . . . It took me right to a fourteen-year-old's summer!! I couldn't put it down."

—BRADY REITER, actress (*100 Things to Do Before High School, Tooth Fairy 2,* and *Just Add Magic*)

"*Saltwater Secrets* is a fast-paced tween mystery, great for a day at the beach."

—ELISE ALLEN, author of *Twinchantment* and coauthor of the series Gabby Duran and the Unsittables

"If you're a fan of *Just Add Magic*, you'll love *Saltwater Secrets*. Another great story filled with mystery and charm! I loved it!"

—AUBREY K. MILLER, actress, dancer, and singer (*Just Add Magic*)

Don't Miss These Great Reads from Cindy Callaghan:

Just Add Magic

Just Add Magic 2: *Potion Problems*

Lost in London

Lucky Me/Lost in Ireland

Lost in Paris

Lost in Rome

Lost in Hollywood

Sydney Mackenzie Knocks 'Em Dead

One

Stella

603 Whalehead Street

June 18

The music on the car radio broke:

> "Murielle duPluie here with the Whalehead news from the Jersey Shore. Welcome to the summer. It's gonna be a hot one today. Stay tuned to WLEO all season for the latest happenings."

My mom stopped in front of 603 Whalehead Street. "Listen, Stell," she said. "Stay out of trouble, okay? If you get a third strike . . . Well, you know."

"I got it, Mom."

She leaned over and kissed me. "Have a great summer. Say hi to Josie for me, and *cawl* me." Mom sounds like me—a total New Yorker. "And text me every single solitary day. And send lots of pictures." She sighed and put her hand on her heart. "Ugh, I miss you *already*." She kissed me again and drove away without saying hello to her first husband, my dad, Gary Higley.

I barely got up the gravel driveway before my sister, Josie, ran out of the house.

"Stellaaaa! You're finally here!"

As soon as I saw Josie, I knew things were going to be different this summer.

Well, Josie herself wasn't different. She seemed exactly the same as last summer, and the one before, and the one before that, right down to the Whalehead T-shirt and gray gym shorts.

That was the problem.

I'd expected the ready-to-enter-high-school version of Josie. After all, I'd become the ready-to-enter-high-school version of me, partly thanks to some new friends who turned out to not really be friends and caused me to get in trouble. Twice.

Well, I guess it wasn't all their fault. Anyway, I couldn't get in trouble this summer, which wouldn't be any problem, because I'd be with Josie, and she never did anything bad.

"G'day, Stella!" Josie hugged me and bounced up and down. "Put your stuff away so we can hit the boardwalk. I'm dying for water ice." With her accent, "ice" sounds like "oyce." When we were kids, and Josie wasn't around, I'd imitate her and tell people I was Australian. "I can't get it at home, you know?"

I hugged her back. "Get outta here. I'm sure they have water ice somewhere—it's a big country."

"Oh, it's not the same," Josie said, and trailed behind me as she wheeled my suitcase into the house. "Whose shorts are those?"

I looked down at my cutoffs. "They're mine. You like them?"

She poked at the skin that was just at the frayed hemline of my shorts. "They are definitely . . . cheeky!"

"It's supposed to be that way." I'd worn these shorts a hundred times and never felt self-conscious before, but now I wondered if my butt really did show too much.

Dad met us in the living room. "Stella! Where have you been? We've been waiting and waiting." He smooshed my face into his chest. I saw Dad pretty much every other weekend, except when I had activities in the city that I didn't want to miss, but he always acted like it'd been forever.

"Mom stopped to pee like ten times."

He grabbed Josie, too, and squeezed the three of us together. "My girls!" He let us go so that he could study us. "So grown-up, but you still look like you could be twins." It was an old joke, because we don't look anything alike; we're both clones of our mothers: Josie is blond and blue eyed, and I'm brown hair and eyes and always tan.

I punched his chest. "You're still working out. Did you show Josie?"

He flexed his arms. "Check out these puppies." His arms weren't quite "puppies." "I'm no-carbing this summer, gonna get ripped."

"Sounds like a good plan." I looked at the tackle box by the front door. "Gonna get ripped while you're fishing?"

"I work out in the morning and fish in the afternoon. At night, I'm gonna try the dating thing. My friend Jay—he's the one that's the detective—is setting it up."

Josie slapped her hands over her ears. "Ugh. I'm *not* listening to you talk about dating, Dad."

I actually thought it was a good idea. "Looking for Mrs. Higley number three?"

"Only if she's looking for me." He winked and glanced at his watch. "I wish you'd gotten here earlier, Stell. Sorry, but I gotta run. Jay's waiting at the dock for me. He's taking me out on his boat, and I'm holding him up."

"That's okay. We can hang out later," I said.

"Not just later. A lot. I have big plans for us to do tons of stuff together." He picked up his tackle box and opened the door. "I'll make us dinner—prepare yourself for my famous steamed broccoli."

I caught a look from Josie, and I knew she wanted me to say something. "We might get pizza."

"Yeah," Josie agreed. "I've been looking forward to it for weeks. I can't get good pizza in Australia."

"Okay," he said. "But after that, we're starting game one of a Monopoly tournament, so don't make other plans."

"For sure," she said, then added, "I love Monopoly."

I was less enthusiastic. I'd hoped to graduate from board games to bonfires on the beach with cute lifeguards and new friends.

Dad grabbed his fishing pole, and, just before shutting the door behind him, he said, "Same deal as always. Text me at nine, twelve, and three o'clock, and be home by six for dinner."

"Yup," we said together.

"Got it, Stell?"

"I got it."

He closed the door.

"What was that about?" Josie asked about the extra "Got it, Stell?"

I shrugged. "Oh, nothing. He worries, you know."

So, about my dad. He's been married twice. First to my mom, Montana—they got divorced before she knew she was pregnant with me. As soon as they separated, he met Kate. It was love at first sight. They got married after just a few dates, moved to Australia to be close to Kate's family, and had Josie, only four months after I was born. Turned out that Gary Higley's dream of love at first sight fizzled in the outback.

Dad returned to New Jersey. Now one daughter (me) lives in New York City with my mom and my stepdad, while his other daughter (Josie) is in Sydney with her mom and her stepdad. The three of us are together for only eight weeks each summer.

I was glad Dad was interested in dating again. He deserved to be happy, but I didn't love the idea of him getting remarried. I mean, I had to share Mom, and I didn't want to share him, too.

"So, what's up, Jo?" I asked. "Get me caught up on your life."

There was no answer, because she wasn't there. I looked around. Neither was my suitcase.

"Josie?"

She popped her head out of the bedroom we shared. "Putting your stuff in here so summer can begin. You can unpack later, yeah?"

"Sure," I said. "I just need to look at the ocean to feel like I'm really here." I walked onto the back porch that overlooked the Atlantic. I loved the smell of salt in the air and the sound of the rolling waves. It was the complete opposite of the concrete and traffic of home.

My dad had inherited this house from his parents and carried on the tradition of spending summers here. It's perfect that he's a teacher, so we can come down here.

If not for these weeks at the shore, Josie and I would

hardly ever see each other. After all, she lives literally on the other side of the world.

This tradition was so important to both of us that once we got cell phones, we made a pact: Except for moms, we wouldn't contact our non-summer worlds while we were in Whalehead. It was hard for me not to call Pete, my best friend and crush forever, but I'd done it. This year it wouldn't be hard at all.

"Ready for water ice?" she asked.

"Have I ever *not* wanted water ice?" It was our tradition to kick off the summer witha trip to Water Ice World. There was no reason that this year's trip would be any different.

Two

Stella

Police Station

June 25

The detective stands by the door of an interview room and says to my dad, "Gary, I'll be happy to listen before any sort of official questioning begins, and it probably will, from what I understand. You can join us in here."

"What about a lawyer?" Dad asks Detective Santoro.

"Always a good idea. I can give you some names, and you can make calls while I talk to her, if you want."

"Nah, that's all right," Dad says. "I know who to call."

"Are you sure you wanna call him?" the detective asks.

Dad is referring to my stepdad, Gregory—not Greg. He's nice enough, I guess. Just weird about his name, and he kind of changed my world—which had been perfectly fine—when he entered it.

"Yeah." Dad sighs. "I'm sure." Then Dad adds, "And, Jay, thanks."

"Don't thank me yet. And you know, I can't pull any strings or anything."

"I'm not asking you to. I just want you to listen to the whole story and tell me what you think."

"Yup," the detective says. "Can do."

Dad looks at me. "Just tell Detective Santoro what happened. I'll be right out here. You just give me the signal if you need me."

I nod with a half smile, because our traditional "signal" is for me to tuck my hands under my armpits and flap like chicken wings.

Santoro closes the door. It's incredibly quiet in here. He waves me to a chair.

"Comfortable?" he asks me.

"Sure," I say, but actually I'm cold under the air-conditioning vent, and the room is anything but comforting—dull white walls without so much as a clock, dirty laminated floor on which there might be dots of blood.

Santoro sits across the metal table from me. The table is distressed with scratches and dents.

He indicates a mirror. "You can't see or hear your dad, but he can see and hear you."

"Okay." I have nothing to hide. I mean, everything we did was for the right reason. He'll understand once he hears the whole story.

"I may take some notes, but they're just for me."

I nod.

"What's your name?"

"Stella Higley." Because I'm from New York, sometimes it sounds like I'm saying "Stellar," but I deliberately leave the r sound off.

"Right. I remember. The other one is the Aussie."

"Yeah, Josie." Then I ask, "Hey, any word from the hospital?"

"Not yet."

"I hope she's okay."

"From what I understand, you did what you could," he says.

I nod.

Santoro says, "We can stop anytime you want, and of course, you know you're free to leave anytime you want." The tone of his voice doesn't sound like he means that, but he probably uses that voice all day with criminals and doesn't know how to change it.

"Yeah."

"Start from the beginning, when you first arrived in Whalehead this summer."

I say to the detective, "We set out for the boardwalk, but Josie didn't change from her T-shirt and gym shorts."

He replies, "Thanks for the wardrobe details, but that's not relevant."

"It is, though," I explain. "Because it bothered me. It shouldn't have, but it did."

"Her outfit bothered you?"

"It really did," I confirm. "It told me she was still eighth-grade Josie, and, I mean, I was nearly-high-school Stella. Another season of riding the Minotaur Coaster wasn't gonna cut it for me."

Santoro studies me, then asks, "So, what are you saying? You were too cool for her?"

"Whoa, I didn't say that." I think for a hot sec. "Well, maybe." I don't like the idea of someone thinking that I think that I'm too cool for Josie. "Except that saying it that way sounds terrible. It makes me sound mean or something, and I'm not."

His face remains flat. I don't know if that's just his face, like he doesn't have other expressions, or if he doesn't believe me.

"I'm really not," I assure him. "I love Josie. I just wanted different things this summer. Is that so bad?"

"Look, Stella, I'm sorry you and your half sister had some tension, but that's not relevant to this very serious situation."

"I think it is."

He stretches his neck right and left until he gets it to crack. "How so?"

"If things had gone the way I'd wanted them to, we would've been busy with bonfires and lifeguards." I add, "The disconnect between Josie and me . . . it's the reason this all started. The sitch on the pier was something we were both interested in. We were both excited about it. And we needed that."

"Understood. But let's get back to the facts that put someone into the hospital." He looks at his watch. "Stella, we don't have a lot of time, so please stick to the facts."

"Okay, but can I officially state something important for the record?"

"You can, but understand that this isn't official."

"Gotcha." Then, as calmly and maturely as I can, I say, "It was all my idea. Everything. Josie didn't have anything to do with it."

Three

Stella

Boardwalk

June 18 (Continued)

Josie and I set out for our ritual: water ice and then the fun house, which is the building right next door to Water Ice World. Between the two buildings is a wooden ramp that goes from Thirty-Fourth Street to the beach.

On the way, Josie filled me in on life down under: "I'm super busy with my school's marine conservation society. I'm running for prez in the fall, so excited about that." Josie also does this Aussie thing where she shortens words as much as they can possibly be. "Sea turtles are espesh a big issue."

"President sounds like a big deal. Good luck. Maybe I can work on some posters for you. My digital design has gotten pretty good."

"That'd be great, Stell. Thanks."

"How's your mom?" I asked.

"Mum is Mum."

Talk about a non-answer. I wondered what was up with that; instead of asking, I said, "Sea turtles are the cutest. Good thing they have your help."

She nodded. "How's Greg?"

I corrected her. "Gregory."

"Right."

"He's good. Nice. The apartment feels different with him in it. It's like there's always a guest around. My mom and I never just lie around in jammies anymore, you know?" I asked. "But sometimes it's good, like when he makes pancakes or drives me places."

"Change is hard, at least for me. Maybe he won't feel like a guest after a while." That was easy for her to say. Her mom, Kate, got remarried when Josie was a baby, so she's only known life with her stepdad in the house. Plus he's a surfer, which is very cool.

"Maybe," I said. What I didn't say out loud was that I liked it better when it was just me and Mom. And I felt guilty that I felt that way, because why shouldn't she be able to get remarried? I was just about to change the convo and ask Josie if she had a boyfriend, and maybe tell her about Pete, when the sight of Water Ice World made us freeze.

It was gone.

In its place was something called the Smoothie Factory. And the place was jam-packed.

"What the heck?" I said. The Smoothie Factory buzzed with people, music, bright lights, and color. If I hadn't seen the name, I might've guessed it was a dance club with an eighties neon theme.

"It's like the end of an era," Josie added.

Just then we heard a familiar "HELL-o!" And there was Alayna Appleton, an inch from our faces.

Alayna, aka the Amazing Apple, was a thirteen-year-old magician. Her MO was to troll the boardwalk and beach, sharing card tricks and pulling arcade tokens out of people's ears, noses, and butts. She was popular among vacationers, especially kids, and she'd cornered the babysitting market. She had one trick that she reserved specifically for me, Josie, and our other shore friend, Dario. Most magicians pride themselves on their ability to disappear, but the Amazing Apple wasn't like most magicians.

She was a master at *appearing*. That is, she would materialize inside one of our personal-space bubbles with no warning. It was cute when we were kids, but now it was just creepy. Neither of us liked it, but Alayna was like a song you can't get out of your head—it drives you crazy and it's annoying, but you find yourself singing along, because you also kind of like it at the same time you're wishing it would go away.

Josie jumped. "Alayna, you scared the pants off me."

"I'm going by 'Apple' this year. You know, nearly in high school and all. Time for a whole new brand." She smiled big. "Look. Got my braces off."

Even Alayna was evolving for high school. "Great seeing you, Alayna—I mean, Amazing—I mean, Apple—but we're totally late." I nudged Josie to walk away.

"Guess what?" Apple stopped us.

Neither of us asked what.

"Turns out I'm lactose intolerant." She made an exaggerated pout. "Gives me gas."

Was she really telling us about her gas?

"Bummer," Josie said.

"Guess what else?" Apple asked.

We still didn't ask what, but she said, "This winter I apprenticed with the enchantress of Estonia. So, that's kind of a big deal. She's expert in the act of exorcism and elemental recomposition. Together we scaled the cliffs of Saaremaa Island and called upon necromancing quadrilaterals and—"

"Uh, sounds great." I cut her off. "Sorry. But we're late, remember?"

We'd managed to get a few feet away when Josie turned and called back to her, "See ya." But Apple was gone.

"Maybe the quadrilateral enchanters taught her how to disappear," I said.

"You have to admit," Josie said, "she truly is amazing."

Josie was right, but I'd outgrown magic tricks.

Josie returned to our previous problem and asked, "What if Kevin's Fun House closed too? You know what that would mean? Oh no, Stell, what if . . ."

It sounded like Josie was panicking about the fun house, but she was actually concerned about what we'd hidden there. Well, not *there*. But *under* there. If Kevin's Fun House closed, we'd lose our supercool way to access our hiding spot.

To calm her I said, "There's no way," but she was already racing down the little stretch of boardwalk between the Smoothie Factory and Kevin's Fun House. It was under this part of the boardwalk that was important to us.

"Slow down," I called to Josie. Man, she'd gotten faster, or I'd gotten slower. Probably some of each.

She slowed and noticed I was out of breath from sprinting only a few yards. "I guess you didn't have a great track season this year?"

"Nah. I quit."

"What? Why?"

"It would've totally eaten into my social life," I said.

Josie said, "I thought Pete was your whole social life."

I said, "I branched out this year. I actually had a lot of sleepovers with my friends, and then I was too tired to go to practice because we'd stay up all night. And . . . I had a lot of studying to do." I didn't want to tell her that I'd been asked to leave the track team. Well, okay, so more *told* than *asked*, but she didn't need to know that. "I guess you had a good season?"

"Really good. I'm sorry to hear you gave it up. You loved it."

I shrugged. "It was time for other stuff. It's fine."

Kevin's Fun House was there, same as always, except it didn't look the same. It looked a little tired. The paint on the slide was fading in the middle, and the *v* in Kevin's name had come loose and hung to the side, like <.

"Ready to give it a checkout?" Josie asked

"Let's do it," I said.

Josie gave me one of the VIP wristbands that Dad'd bought for us so we could skip the line. I noticed that we were the tallest of the kids waiting. We headed in, stopped at the hall of mirrors, many of which were cloudy and cracked, and looked at ourselves. I'd seen these reflections a hundred times before, so it wasn't that funny to me anymore. Then we wiggled through the foam pillars; most had chunks missing, and their previously bright colors had dulled. Lastly, we scaled the rope bridge, which I could now get over with one step. Unfortunately, I tripped on that one step because my sandal got caught.

Josie arrived at the barrel first.

"I win," she crowed.

"It wasn't a race."

"It's always a race," Josie said. "Every single time we come here, we've raced to this exact barrel."

I didn't respond. She was right, of course, but I didn't feel like racing, and I didn't want to argue about it. Instead, I looked around. "All clear."

Josie stomped and popped up the chunk of loose floorboards. "What will we do if Kevin ever decides to fix this?" Josie asked, and before I could answer, she disappeared through the hole.

I jumped next, pulling our trapdoor shut behind us.

Four

Stella

Under the Boardwalk
June 18 (Continued)

We dropped about five feet to the sand below, plopping onto our butts. Sand wiggled up inside my shorts into places where I would've preferred not to have sand.

We studied our hideaway. I was always struck by its stuffiness. When stuffy and beach mix, it smells like dead fish. *Yuck.* It was shady, except for where sunlight snuck through the cracks between the boards above. In some of those sandy patches, tufts of beach grass grew. Overhead we could hear all sorts of boardwalk activity: people laughing, biking, and skateboarding, even though they're not supposed to.

I had great memories of being down here. One time there was a huge storm, and we curled up and told each other scary stories and watched lightning bolts spike at the ocean, until we heard Dad frantically calling our names from the beach. He was so relieved when he found us that he forgot he was mad at us.

"It looks different," Josie said.

There used to be a latticed fence on the ocean side that went from the boardwalk to the sand, hiding us from beach-goers. We could see through the crisscrosses. The fence had been replaced with a sliding door that hung from rails, the kind you'd see on a barn.

"What's with that?" Josie pointed to a deep groove in the sand. It started at the new sliding door and crossed the sand alley under the boardwalk between Kevin's Fun House and what was now the Smoothie Factory. The groove went toward the opening to Thirty-Fourth Street.

I said, "It looks like a bigger version of the kind of groove that kids dig in the sand as a river." Those never really work, because the water soaks into the sand before it reaches its intended place—probably a castle moat. But there were no castles down here.

Josie said, "And check out all the footies." Josie meant footprints. "People have been hanging out down here. And I don't see our marker."

I brushed the sand around in the spot where I remembered the rock being, then dug with my hands. "No rocks. No box," I said. "It's gone."

"Gone? Gone!" Josie cried. "First Water Ice World, now this?" She frantically dug deeper. When she didn't find anything, she sat in the sand. "Those memories are just gone!" She looked at me. "Why aren't you upset? You should be upset about this, Stella!"

"I am," I said. "But I mean, maybe it's a sign."

"What kind of a sign would take away our treasures?'"

"A sign that we should make new memories. You know, have a different kind of summer. We could do that."

"I thought you loved it the way it was! What's wrong with the way it's always been, Stella?" Josie yelled. Her ice-blue eyes weren't far from tears.

I said, "We could make a new box. Maybe hide it someplace where the sand doesn't go up our butts, and we don't hit our heads when we stand up all the way." There was about five feet between the sand and the boardwalk. Last year we started having to hunch over when we walked down here. "Or maybe we don't have to hide it? We could keep it at Dad's."

"I don't like that idea at all, and, Stella, that box was very special to me."

"It was to me, too," I said, and I meant it, but I mean, it was *a box*. "Just because the box is gone doesn't mean those things didn't happen."

Something else caught Josie's eye. "Oh great. That's changed too." She pointed to the door that had led to the Water Ice World basement. It was now painted lime green and had a shiny new lock. "We can't get back up top the way we used to." Yasmina, the owner of Water Ice World, hadn't minded that we'd cut through her store. In fact, she'd liked that we were so comfortable with the place that we'd let ourselves in. She'd said we were practically family. "Now I hate that smoothie place even more."

We checked out our options: Once the trapdoor to the fun house was closed, it couldn't be opened from down here. So I went to the sliding door and pulled on it to try to access the beach, but it, too, was locked.

Our last resort was to walk through the sandy alley between the Smoothie Factory and Kevin's Fun House toward Thirty-Fourth Street, which wasn't really a big deal. It was just a longish walk to the pavement, then down the street a bit to the ramp that led back to the boardwalk; that's the way we went.

Coincidentally, it was the same direction the groove went—from the beach to Thirty-Fourth Street.

What was with that groove?

Five

Stella

Police Station

June 25 (Continued)

"So the missing box . . . ," Santoro says at the same time as he thumbs something on his phone.

"That darn box. I wanted to be excited to go find it, and I wanted to be more upset that it was gone, but the truth is, it didn't bother me that much. I mean, it did a little, but not as much as it upset Josie. I tried to act upset. I wanted to be upset, because if I wasn't, Josie would be upset, and I didn't want that."

Santoro sighs. "I was going to ask if you knew what happened to it."

"No. It's just gone. I guess stolen or somehow washed out to sea."

"And this magic girl . . ." He flips to a new page.

"Alayna. The Amazing Apple," I say.

"Right. You said she had a knack for simply appearing without warning?"

"That's right. Right into your personal space. And she'd talk real close to your face. Like this." I lift myself from my chair and position my nose an inch from his and tilt my head ever so slightly. He has deep creases in the corners of his eyes and between them, like his brows spend a lot of time in a furrowed position. Probably he squints at clues and suspects.

"Close talker. I got it," he says. "You can sit back down, Stella."

I add, "And you can always smell the last thing she'd eaten." I sit. "Usually a tuna sandwich. Who eats tuna at the beach?"

"How did she stealthily appear like that?"

"Magic, I guess." I shrug. "She says she's studied all over the world, but I don't buy it. She always tells us about the exotic places she's gone and the techniques she's learned from practicing wizards. I'm waiting for the day that she brings up Dumbledore. Then I'll know she's full of it."

He doesn't smile at that. What kind of a guy doesn't smile at a spontaneous Dumbledore reference? How does my dad spend all day on a boat with this guy? He's as personable as a doorknob.

I get on with the story in the hopes that our time together can come to a quick end. But then again, what if Santoro ends up being the only thing that stands between me and handcuffs?

Six

Stella

Boardwalk
June 18 (Continued)

Once we were back on the boardwalk, I faced into the wind, let it blow my hair out of my sweaty face, and I tied my hair into a knot on the top of my head. Josie didn't get as hot as I did, and her blond hair wasn't quite long enough to top-knot.

"Where to now?" Josie asked.

I looked at everyone slurping from lime-green cups. "I wanna check out those smoothies."

"You can't be serious?" Josie asked. "You're gonna buy something from that factory? They're, like, the enemy."

"You're being a little extra, Jo. It's just a smoothie. It isn't going to hurt anything."

"I'll wait in line with you, but I'm not having any." She added, "I'm officially boycotting."

The line was out the door. As we waited, I studied the place through the window. The walls were painted bright lime green, and metal baskets of fresh fruit hung from chains. Employees in white lab coats put peeled and cut chunks of fruit into clear tubes that led to blenders. Customers put their lime-green cups under the spigots coming from the blenders. They filled their cups with blended, drinkable fruit and stirred them with long, orange spoons. There was a self-serve bar where people could scoop on healthy toppings like granola and diced figs.

"It's so ug," Josie said, meaning "ugly," but I thought the colors and white coats really brightened the place.

We still hadn't made it inside when three familiar faces came out. Two out of the three held branded lime-green cups.

"G'day," Josie greeted them.

"Welcome to the shore," TJ said, holding my eyes for a hot sec longer than Josie's. We could file TJ under things that had definitely changed. He was about a foot taller than last year, and his voice was deeper.

"It's about time," Tucker said.

"Where ya been?" Timmy asked.

TJ, Tucker, and Timmy—or the Three *T*s, as we called them—were the same age as us, thirteen. They were a trio of best summer friends who lived in different towns during the year, but were glued at the hip at the shore. This year they wore matching red T-shirts that said GUARD on the back, although they weren't full lifeguards yet; they were in training. The real lifeguards wore white shirts with red letters.

You'd think that, being called the Three *T*s and wearing matching shirts, they might be triplets, but they were far from clones. Three different backgrounds, three different personalities, yet still best friends—at least for the summer.

"Hey there," I said, mostly to TJ, whose dark curly hair was already sun-pecked with highlights. "We just got here. After this we were heading to the lifeguard shack to see what's going on tonight."

Josie asked, "We were?"

No one seemed to notice her question.

TJ said, "We got some stuff planned. I think the first bon—"

"Hold up," Josie said. "Before we get to the summer schedule, what's with *this* place?" I suspected Josie's "hold up" interrupted what was going to be an invitation to a bonfire. *That* was an invitation I wanted, and I was frustrated that she might've just made us lose it.

"Uh . . ." I tried to stop her from "holding up" so TJ could finish, but Josie was steamed about the Smoothie Factory, and she wanted the guys to know it.

"I can't believe you're eating that." She glanced at their cups—Timmy's and TJ's—with a snarl. "Or drinking? Is it a food or a drink?" She poked at Timmy's long spoon. "If you have a spoon and a straw, I mean, I can't even." To the Three *T*s she asked, "Where's your loyalty to Water Ice World?"

None of them answered right away. I think maybe they were afraid of saying the wrong thing, which they probably would have.

TJ bravely gave it a try. "I'll eat anywhere. I don't discriminate."

Josie said, "I'm not discriminating. I'm *protesting*. There's a difference."

I decided to lighten the mood. I asked TJ, "Is it good?"

He held his cup out for me, and I took a sip.

"Mmm." I wiped a little green mustache off with my index finger, then tipped my sunglasses down to examine Timmy's cup. "Crushed walnut?"

"Extra protein," he said. "We have some seriously tough fitness goals to meet for the program this summer." Then he asked Josie, "You still running?"

"Oh, yeah," she said.

"Maybe we can run somewhere," he said.

She replied, "I jogged on the beach last night, before Stella got here. The sun was going down, and the sand had cooled off. You should try that."

I was pretty sure Timmy had meant "run together," but

Josie definitely missed that cue. I asked Tucker, "Why didn't you get a smoothie?"

Tucker said, "I have a policy to never touch green drinks. They gimme the heebie-jeebies. Drinks should be white, brown, or pink—vanilla, chocolate, or strawberry. Not green. As far as food goes, I prefer things that have been fried, flipped, scooped, dipped in chocolate, or put in a tortilla shell." He shrugged. "I'm a picky eater, I guess."

"If you don't start picking better things, you're not gonna keep up with our training," Timmy warned.

"I've got these." Tucker lifted an arm and said, "Bam!" when he flexed it, then "Bam!" when he flexed the other one. "I'm the only guard who can bench a whale, so, yeah, there's that."

While I didn't totally believe the whale part, I had to admit Tuck had really big arm muscles.

TJ shook his head at Tucker and asked me, "You gonna get some?"

"Yup," I said.

"No," Josie snapped.

Timmy licked smoothed banana off his spoon and said to Josie, "You're missing out." He held the cup out to her. "Sure you don't want to try it?"

She pressed her lips together and shook her head.

"Suit yourself," Timmy said. "Trust me, it's good."

TJ tipped his cup back to get the last drops. "Totally," he added.

"Catch you later?" Timmy asked Josie, who was too busy scanning Smoothie Factory customers with disgust to hear.

"Yeah," I answered for her.

The Three *T*s started walking away: two *T*s toward the guard shack and one *T* toward Sam's Soft-Serve iScream.

TJ turned back to me, and I thought he was going to drop the bonfire invite. Instead he held up his phone. "You still have the same number?"

I nodded.

"I'll text you," he said.

I nodded again. Now, that felt different and a lot more like I wanted to feel this summer.

"I can't even believe them," Josie said, oblivious to Timmy wanting to catch her later, or TJ planning to text me, or nearly getting invited to a bonfire.

Then we saw Dario heading toward us. "I can't believe *this*!" His face was lit up like a kid realizing it was the last day of school before spring break. He held out a paper flyer.

We gave him a quick hello hug, then read the flyer.

And he was right; it was unbelievable.

Seven

Stella

Police Station

June 25 (Continued)

"Now we also have these three boys. . . ." Santoro flips a page in his spiral notebook and goes to write down their names, like he's trying to keep track of all the players here.

He writes T*, then* T*, then* T*, and pauses. Then I say, "One of them, Timmy, liked Josie; I could tell right away. And I got a vibe from TJ that he was interested in me. You know what I mean?"*

He doesn't write anything down, because he doesn't know what I mean.

"Interested," I repeat. "Like liked *me."*

That does it. He turns the page. I have to hold back a laugh, because it seems Santoro can question hardened criminals, throw the book at them, and probably rough them up, even set Dad up on a blind date, but he can't hear about my crush, which is just what I hoped for, because I don't want to talk to him about anything else involving the Three Ts.

"Tell me about Dario," Santoro says.

I have no problem telling him all about Dario, because I don't have to keep him out of trouble. "He's our shore friend. We've hung out with him every year since we were kids. I can't even remember how we first met. Josie probably would; she remembers everything."

I continue, "Dario lives at the shore all year, so he knows all about what happens in the off-season, and he gives us the scoop. He works at the Nifty Gifty. It's one of the few jobs that's year-round, and his parents know the owners, so they let him help out, even though he's thirteen, like us. Most places want you to be fifteen or sixteen. He said he could get us jobs there next summer, but I don't think I'd like it. I'd rather work at the surf shop. Josie wants to get her lifeguard certification at home this winter and guard next year. I wish I could do that, but I'm not a strong enough swimmer. It would be great for us socially if Josie was a guard, because then we'd always know what was going on, although I would probably gather a lot of that info at the surf shop. Who knows, really? The jury is still out on that, but you know all about juries."

I think Santoro stopped listening to me around "lifeguard certification." He pushes his shoulders back to get a good stretch. I wonder if he was in some altercation with a criminal that left his neck and back achy.

When I stop talking about jobs, he raises his brows as if signaling me to say more.

"Dario doesn't like working at Nifty. He wants to be a newscaster. In fact, one day he wants Murielle duPluie's job. Do you know her?"

He writes something down, maybe Dario's name, but I can't decipher his terrible handwriting. Or maybe it's code that only detectives understand. Then he looks at me. "No," he says like I've irritated him by asking a question. I guess when you're being interviewed by a detective, they're the only ones allowed to ask questions.

The room is quiet for a hot sec. That's when my stomach chooses to growl. It must be past dinnertime by now.

He brings me back to the story. "So, the flyer. What was so unbelievable?"

Eight

Stella

Boardwalk

June 18 (Continued)

I looked at the flyer advertising a concert. Not any concert. The Flying Fish were coming to Whalehead and would play on Murphy's Pier.

Josie, Dario, and I, and pretty much everyone else on the planet, *loved* the Flying Fish. The lead singer, Meredith Maxwell, was the best. She was a great singer, and not much older than us, which was cool.

"She's so pretty," Josie said.

"What do you think they'll play first?" Dario asked. "I'm betting on 'Wrap Me in Tentacles.' Wanna bet? Let's make a bet."

Josie said, "I think it'll be 'World Is Your Oyster.' But I don't wanna bet."

"Chicken," Dario taunted, then added, "I'd like to have tentacles for a day or a week to see what it's like." He pulled his phone out of his back pocket and made himself a voice memo. "Future news segment: What's the deal with tentacles? Reporter spends a day swapping arms and legs for tentacles."

Josie asked, "Why stop there? What about fins and gills?"

"Good ideas, Jo."

This banter lasted until we made it to the Smoothie Factory's self-serve counter. I flicked the spigots of the tubes carrying mango, kiwi, and pineapple. Each fruit was its own magnificent color with thin ribbons of purple twirling through it.

"What's the purple?" Josie asked.

Dario said, "That's the stuff that makes these über-healthy. Their secret sauce. Murielle duPluie did a story. The nutritional value is off the charts."

I sprinkled coconut on top, stirred it with a long orange spoon, and finally tested it. "Like a tropical wonder. Wanna try?" I held it out for them.

"No thanks," Josie said. "I can't even look at it."

Dario took a sip while Josie led us back outside to the boardwalk and returned to our previous topic as we strolled down the boards.

Josie said, "The Flying Fish will be *the* event of the summer. People will come from all over. This pier will be packed."

That's when we saw Rodney leaning on the boardwalk railing across from the Smoothie Factory entrance, waxing his surfboard. He said, "It'll be a disaster."

Rodney was a slightly eccentric shore fixture, with a long scraggly beard and a dark tan that seeped deep into his wrinkles and blurred his aging tattoos. He lived to surf, and surfing was his life. When he wasn't in the water, he was researching any variety of conspiracies ranging from little green men, to the secret society controlling the world, to the faked moon landing. We didn't buy into them, but they were entertaining conversation on rainy days, and he was always nice to us.

"G'day, Mr. Rodney." Josie looked at the lime-green cup set by his feet. "Not you, too?"

"I had to sample it." He shrugged. "It ain't half-bad. And I'm not getting any younger, so I can use the vitamins. You know your run-of-the-mill produce can't yield these kinds of nutrition numbers, so it makes you wonder what's really in it."

"More like it makes *you* wonder," I said. "The rest of us just like drinking it."

"Not all of us," Josie clarified.

"I get your drift, Jo. I truly do, mate." Rodney always called Josie "mate." Not only that, but he nailed the accent. Australians say long *a*'s as a long *i*. They also add a little "oy" wherever they can. So whenever Josie said "mate," it came out, "mite." And that was how Rodney said it.

"Girls, mark my words on this one. . . ." Rodney was always marking his words, so that when the truth eventually came out about something, like, for example, that Zac Efron was actually an alien, we'd remember that he'd predicted it. "If something can pack this much nutrition into this much cup"—he held up the cup—"we need to ask how."

"How?" I asked.

He didn't answer right away while he stared out at the ocean with a combination of love, respect, and awe that resembled the way an old man might look back on his life. "She holds many tales," he said.

I guessed he'd forgotten that we were talking about smoothie nutrition facts and had moved on to ocean awe. "Sure does," I said.

"Lots of tales," Dario agreed.

"What are we talking about? Buried treasure? Pirates?" Josie asked. "Or marine species? Because *that's* my specialty."

Rodney didn't address Josie's questions. Instead he pointed to the flyer and asked, "So, Meredith Maxwell's coming here of all places. Why Whalehead, New Jersey?"

At the mention of Meredith Maxwell, we catapulted questions:

"Can you even believe it?"

"What do you think she'll open with?"

"Think we can get into the front row?"

Again, Rodney's mind had already shifted to the next thing. He used his chin to indicate Murphy's Pier, home of the fabulous Minotaur Coaster. "I love that thing." Then he did something bizarre, even by Rodney standards: He took a ziplock bag out of a duffel that sat at his feet. He poured the last drops of the smoothie into it, sealed it shut with a pinch, and put it back into the duffel. Then he tossed his empty green cup into the trash can. Next, he swung the duffel over his shoulder, grabbed his surfboard, and lifted it over his head. He said to us, "The ocean is calling, mates. And I must answer."

He walked down the ramp to the sand, dropped the bag, and switched to a jog. Once he hit the water, he belly flopped on top of the board and arm-paddled over the white-capped waves.

"I think that guy gets too much sun," I said. "Messes with his brain cells."

While we were talking, Josie's alarm on her phone went off. Time to check in with Dad. She sent a super-quick text and flashed me the screen so I could see what she'd done.

It also gave me a chance to glance at my own phone to see if TJ had texted. He hadn't.

Without missing a beat, Josie asked Dario, "What's his story?" Dario has the backstory on everyone, like a future news reporter should.

"He was a scientist in a former life. He invented something that helps with something and made a ton of money. He retired to live the life of his dreams, as a surf bum."

"He's rich?" I confirmed.

"Filthy. Most people don't know that. They also don't realize that he's way smarter than he may seem."

Nine

Stella

Police Station

June 25 (Continued)

There's a knock on the door.

"Excuse me," Santoro says. The chair makes a terrible screech when he pushes it back. He straightens himself up slowly, and the grimace on his face says he hurts. I wonder if maybe he got shot in the back or something.

He peeks his head out the door but doesn't actually leave.

I'm pleasantly surprised when chips and soda appear. I guess I assumed he'd engage in hushed detective whispers about me or some other case, but he was getting us a snack.

He puts a soda down, pops the top with one big hand, and slides it to me. Then he does the same with the other one for himself. He takes a gulp that probably sucks in half the can.

He drops a bag of chips in front of me, eases back into his chair, crosses his legs, and rips his bag open. He's all settled in to hear the rest of my story. He asks, "You knew Rodney before this day on the boardwalk?"

I sip the Coke. It's warm. "Oh yeah. We've known him for years, but we really still don't know him that well. He's someone that we could talk about for hours."

Santoro sets a chip in his mouth, a whole chip at once, not a bite of a chip. "Why?"

"He's unusual."

"Unusual how?"

"Maybe a better word is 'interesting,'" I clarify. "I like him. We have fun listening to him, but we never really took him seriously."

"But this time you did," Santoro says.

"At this point we had no idea what he was talking about, which was typical, and we really didn't give it a second thought." I add, "It was Rodney gibberish: vitamins, sea tales, and loving the pier. It seemed like nonsense. We didn't fit it together until later."

"What about the part about Meredith Maxwell? Had he mentioned her to you before?" He takes another gulp, finishing the can. He crushes it in his fist and tosses it into the trash can that seriously needs to be emptied.

"No. That was the first time. But it didn't seem strange, because it was a really big deal that she was coming to Whalehead, so it didn't seem odd that he would mention it. Most people are fans, so why wouldn't he be?"

Santoro just sits there staring at me, not saying anything. The silence is painful. It makes me want to blurt out anything to fill it. This is probably how he gets criminals to confess. I have to fill the silence. "At that point, we assumed he was a fan. We didn't know why he was interested in her until later."

"Yeah?"

I'm not sure if that's a question exactly, but I treat it like one. "Yeah. Not until days later. Do you want me to jump ahead to that?"

Santoro drops another chip into his mouth. "Let's stick to the timeline."

Ten

Stella

Murphy's Pier

June 19

The music blared through overhead speakers on Murphy's Pier. The station was WLEO, of course. There was a break between songs:

> "Murielle duPluie from WLEO here with the Whalehead news from the Jersey Shore. Hold on to your hats, beachgoers, because a bounty of bouncy bungee is coming to Murphy's Pier. You can jump, flip, and fly to your heart's content, all with the safety of a harness and blow-up mat to break your fall. Look for this bad boy to rock Whalehead this week."

That next night on the pier was chilly. I wore a cute, lightweight cotton Free People pullover. Josie wanted to wear a crew-neck sweatshirt with the name of her middle school track team, but I talked her into an on-trend crochet sweater I'd brought. We were on our way to high school, and if I was going to have an on-the-way-to-high-school summer, we had to look like it, right?

On the short walk from the house to the pier, we each called our moms.

Gregory answered my mom's phone. "Hey, girl. We miss you."

There was nothing wrong with him saying that, but all I could think was *ugh*. That's always the first thought that comes to mind. "Me too. I mean, I miss you guys too. Can I talk to my mom?"

"Sure. Talk to you again soon, Stell," Gregory said. He never had a hint of "ugh" in his voice when he talked to me. And then I caught up with Mom.

When I hung up, Josie asked me, "Did you hear from Dario?"

"No." I texted him right then before I forgot.

The air on the pier smelled of French fries and funnel cake. People bustled about with tickets for rides and answered the calls to "step right up" at the midway games, eager to win a JERSEY STRONG bumper sticker or Hello Kitty plush toy by tossing rings around the neck of a bottle.

Off work at 7. C U then, Dario replied. Then he added, **#NiftyGifty**. And followed it up with a pukey emoji.

"We should wait for him to ride the Minotaur," Josie said.

"Definitely." Dario needed us to sit on either side of him. He hated the ride and screamed the whole time. He's never gone on it without us.

We got popcorn while we waited; because we couldn't escape steamed broccoli two nights in a row, we were hungry. That's when we bumped into Angie Imani. Angie is Dario's older sister who usually blew us off, too cool to hang out with us. But we were almost in high school now, so I hoped things would change.

"Hey, Angie," I said. "What's up?"

She said, "Hi, Jo-Stell." That's what she called us since she could never remember which one of us was which. "What're you guys up to?"

Josie pointed to the Minotaur. "First of many nights on that coaster."

"And later we'll probably catch up with the guards," I said.

"We will?" Josie asked me.

I definitely wanted to go to the bonfire. I'd waited for years to be old enough. I didn't answer Josie but asked Angie, "What're you doing tonight?" I thought maybe she'd want to hang out with us.

She dangled a set of car keys. "I have the Water Sport Adventure van, so I'm heading to Shelter Harbor."

"Oh, right," I said. "You got your license."

"It changes *everything*. It's like ultimate freedom." She

looked past us. "Look who it is," she said at the sight of Dario. "Definitely my cue to leave." She made an *L* with her thumb and finger on her forehead and walked away.

You needed to be invited or have an "in" to go to a lifeguard bonfire. The Three *T*s could be that, but since they were still in training, it was iffy. I thought Angie could be our "in." She was popular and always went to the bonfires. At least she used to.

"How was work?" Josie asked Dario.

He said, "Who really needs another snow globe, right?"

"So right," Josie said, and the two chatted about snow globes and key chains.

Dario asked her, "What's the deal with refrigerator magnets? Can't you think of anything more interesting to collect?"

I didn't hear the details of magnets, because my focus was drawn to Rodney in the distance. Among vacationers shooting water pistols into plastic clowns' mouths, and kids crying because of dropped ice cream cones or stray balloons, he was writing on a clipboard and pushing buttons on a calculator.

"Why so quiet, Stell?" Dario asked.

"Look at him." I directed their attention.

"What's he doing?" Dario asked.

I said, "Let's find out." We walked over to the railing where Rodney diligently worked. "What's up, Mr. Rodney?"

"Structural assessments." He didn't look at us as he continued pushing buttons on the calculator. "I can't talk now. I'm counting."

"Counting what?" Dario asked anyway.

He sighed. "People. Estimating weights of people, crowds of them. Then I'll ultrasonically assess the thickness of the submerged wooden pylon support beams and compare it to the measurements from earlier today to see how the beams are affected by weight. Basic structural-inspection stuff. I do swim-by inspections in the daylight." He wrote something down. "Look, kids, I can't talk right now. Seriously." He turned his back on us and mumbled a bit.

"Oooookay. Rather than unravel those tentacles," Dario said about the mouthful of confusing lingo Rodney had just dropped on us, "let's talk about something more normal, like the line for the Minotaur, which just went down. I'm in the middle seat."

We only had to wait a minute before getting loaded into a coaster car. There was room for four in a car, and somehow Apple ended up in with us despite not having been in line.

She really was an amazing magician.

After the loud snap of the brace locking to hold us in, we were off.

"I hope it doesn't get stuck at the top again," I said. "Remember when that happened last time?"

"Oh yeah," Josie said. "Hottest day of the year."

Dario said, "The top of my legs got so sunburned, they peeled for a week."

"I love when that happens," Apple said. "Sometimes I save the skin in a bag."

"That's kinda gross," I said.

"Kinda," she said. "But not too much."

As we climbed to the coaster's highest point, I pointed something out to Josie. It was Dad, walking away from a food kiosk in the middle of the midway. He was handing a candy apple to a nice-looking woman, although it was kinda hard from this far away to tell anything else about her.

"Date number one?" I yelled to Josie.

"Looks that waaa—"

The rest of her words were lost in the wind as the coaster dropped us at full speed. From there it jerked and whipped us all around the pier and out over the ocean. The wind blowing through my hair was mixed with a combo of Dario's and Josie's screams.

When we were done, we ran down the exit ramp and stopped to catch our breath. I looked over either shoulder, but no sign of Apple.

"*That* was fantab!" Josie said.

We all laughed at ourselves, the state of our hair, and the amount we'd just yelled. I glanced down at my cell phone and saw that a text had arrived. It was from TJ.

Then suddenly we all stopped laughing when something happened that wasn't funny at all.

Eleven

Stella

Police Station

June 25 (Continued)

Santoro tips the chip bag into his mouth and lets the broken chips and crumbs fall in. After a crunch, he crinkles the bag in his fist and pitches it into the trash can. "What happened when you got off the Minotaur?"

"It was a windy, chilly night."

"I got that part. That happens at the shore."

I pause because I know this is going to sound ridiculous. "It moved."

He does his stare thing when he leaves an uncomfortable silence. This time I'm really stubborn, and I don't fill it. It isn't easy, but I hold my tongue by sipping on warm Coke.

He asks, "What moved? The roller coaster?"

"No." I pause. "The pier."

"Moved how?"

"It felt like . . . Imagine the pier was made of rubber. And the waves were strong . . ."

"Because it was windy," he adds, to show me he's following along with my line of thinking.

"Exactly. Big waves, gusts of wind . . . Like, it bent. Or it felt like it was bending."

"And then what?"

"And then it stopped," I say.

He looks at me to say more, and this time I oblige. "I've spent a lot of time on that pier over the years, and I've never felt it move like that before."

"So what did you do?"

"Before I tell you that, aren't you a little curious about my dad and the lady you set him up with?"

"No." He cracks his neck. "Stella, I'm not."

But that straight, serious, unchanged, flat look on his face told me he was at least a little curious.

Twelve

Stella

Murphy's Pier

June 19 (Continued)

"Did you feel that?" I asked Dario and Josie.

"Totally," Josie said.

"What's the deal with that?" Dario asked. "That never happened before."

"Maybe 'cause it's extra windy tonight?" Josie asked.

"Or maybe our equilibrium is off. From the ride. That can really mess with your mind," I said, then studied the crowd. No one seemed alarmed. Had we imagined it?

I felt my phone vibrate. Since I knew no one from home was texting, so no risk of breaking the pact, I checked it.

It was TJ. **Turn around.**

I did and saw the Three *T*s headed our way. I ran my

fingers through my hair, which was surely a wreck following the ride.

I asked them, "Did you guys feel that?" They were now in red GUARD hoodies.

"It was like a tremor," TJ said.

"Or a shake," Tucker added.

"Think an earthquake?" Timmy asked.

"In New Jersey?" I asked. "Does that happen?"

"It's possible," Dario said. He pulled out his phone. "Let's see what the news is reporting."

The Three *T*s disregarded Dario's quest for the truth, clearly not worried if New Jersey had had a Richter scale–worthy event.

TJ said, "It's bonfire time."

"Or what I like to call 'marshmallow time,'" Tucker added.

"You guys coming?" Timmy asked.

Luckily, the tremor wasn't significant enough to break off a chunk of the Jersey coastline or impede our first bonfire. I said, "Of course."

"What's the deal with marshmallows?" Dario asked all of us.

When no one jumped to answer, TJ said, "See you there." He walked away and brushed his arm against mine. It gave me goose bumps.

Dario was looking down at his phone, but the arm brush had been in his peripheral vision. I'm pretty sure he saw, but he didn't say anything.

Once the Three *T*s left, there was an awkward beat between the three of us that I broke. "Dario, what does it say about the earthquake?"

"Murielle duPluie isn't talking about it. She's on top of the news, as you know. If there had been a real tremor, she'd be reporting it." He added, "So, just a fluke."

Officer Booth walked past us and bumped into Josie. "Scuse me, kids." He was aimed right at Rodney, who was standing on the pier's wooden railing. Rodney looked like he was shouting at people, but with the music, midway, wind, waves, and coaster noise, we couldn't hear him.

Nosey, we followed Officer Booth over to Rodney.

"Get down from there before you fall in," Booth yelled at Rodney. "Let's not have any trouble tonight, Hot Rod."

"I'm not breaking any laws. I have the right to assemble," Rodney said. "And, mark my words, these people have a right to know that the structure of this pier is compromised. Compromised! That's right, the more we allow businesses to mess with the marine ecosystem for profit, the more danger we are in!"

"Danger?" Dario asked.

"What businesses?" I asked.

"The marine ecosystem?" Josie yelled.

"See what you've done?" Booth asked. "You're going to cause a panic. Now get down."

"Maybe there needs to be a panic!" Rodney said. "And

this is a peaceful demonstration. Heard of the First Amendment? I'm not hurting anyone."

"I'll tell you this, Rod: If you don't get down, someone's gonna get hurt, and it's not gonna be me."

Rodney looked at the cop from the railing. "Come on, Booth. You know you don't mean that. You and I go way back. And you know I'm right about this." Regardless of his verbal reluctance to get down, Rodney shifted to a squat on the railing. "Just like I was right about that terrestrial beach landing in '02."

"Sure. Remember, you agreed not to talk about that."

"Confidentiality agreements, blah, blah, blah," Rodney said.

Booth grabbed him around his calf. "Lemme help you, 'cause if you fall in, guess who's gonna have to jump in and save you. Me. And that water is cold."

Rodney got his butt to the railing and looked Booth right in the face. "Seriously, Booth, who'd save who from drowning?"

Booth rolled his eyes. "Rod, I'm not in the mood."

Rodney hopped onto the boards. "I can do my work from the beach." He shook his hair out of his face and stomped away.

"Right. Go look for UFOs down there." Then Booth said to us, "Show's over, kids." And he headed toward the snack bar.

"Think there's any truth to his claims about the ecosystem?" Josie asked.

I said, "Probably not. It sounds like typical Rodney ramblings."

"Sounds like he was right about something in 2002, unless Booth was kidding. Maybe everything he says isn't gibberish," Dario noted. "I'm gonna look into what that was."

"And I'm going to snorkel tomorrow and check out the sea life under this pier," Josie said.

Then we heard, "Stella! Josie!" It was Dad, getting onto the Minotaur. He waved and pointed to the lady next to him, smiled, and gave us a thumbs-up. She waved to us too.

"Looks like date number one is going well," Dario said.

Date number one was an attractive woman who looked about Mom's age, wearing a sundress and denim jacket.

"How do you know about that?" I asked.

"He was in Nifty earlier today. You know, guy talk."

"Eww," I said. "I'm a little grossed out that you and my dad are talking about his dating life."

Josie agreed. "Me too."

The snap of the Minotaur safety bars was audible through the wind; then *click, click, click,* the coaster climbed to the highest point to start the ride. And then *swoosh,* the cart dropped and jerked into the big turn on which the rails actually hang over the side of the pier.

Josie said, "Suddenly the Minotaur seems extra scary when you think that the coaster is supported by a base that could be . . . 'compromised.'"

Dario stared at the wild, jerking ride. "Yup."

Thirteen

Stella

Police Station

June 25 (Continued)

"It sounds like Dario and Josie were more concerned than you about Rodney's claim. Was that the case?"

I think. "Maybe I was a little more realistic that the pier wasn't on the cusp of sinking and that the world as we knew it would be okay if we went to a bonfire." I add, "And I figured we could try to talk to Booth when he was in a better mood. You know Booth?"

"Not well, but I would agree that he's moody."

I smile at that comment, but Santoro doesn't. It seems he only has one mood—serious, flat, frowny, achy.

I say, "Then we made a plan for the next day. Me and Josie were going to snorkel under the pier and check out the eco-

system. Josie has lots of snorkeling experience, which is good, or she might've missed those clues. She's in a group at her school, the marine conservation society, so she knows all about sea life. She's running for president of the group in the fall. It's major. She has to keep her record real clean to be eligible."

Santoro writes something down and quickly turns the page before I can see what it is.

"Okay. So you went to the bonfire next?" he asks.

"We didn't go straight there."

"Where did you stop on the way?"

"On the beach. Something happened that rattled Dario, so it took a few minutes to calm him down."

Fourteen

Stella

Beach

June 19 (Continued)

I kicked off my flip-flops and walked toward the music and sparks from the bonfire. The sand was cold between my toes, which added to my little chill of excitement to finally be going to a bonfire, and to see TJ again. I hadn't even thought about liking a boy besides Pete . . . maybe ever.

"Tell me again why we're going here?" Josie asked. She was borderline whiny, and I wasn't a fan of that.

"It's what people do at the beach, Josie. They listen to music, and dance on the beach, and make s'mores at bonfires. It'll be fun." Then I added, "Timmy will be there."

She didn't seem to pick up on that little hint I dropped about Tim.

"I have to admit, I've always wanted to go to—" Dario screamed and fell onto the sand.

"What's wrong?" I yelled, and bent down to see him.

Josie shouted, "What happened? Should I call nine-one-one?"

Dario grabbed his foot. "I think Mr. Rodney was right. There's extraterrestrial life down here. I think I just stepped on a slimy alien, or its exoskeleton, or intestines."

Josie looked at the sand near Dario. "It's a dead jelly. It happens all the time. Did it sting you?"

"Sting? No, I don't think so. But it's wet and jellied and yuck." He rolled in the sand like he'd been punched in the belly.

"Come on, mate—don't be a baby," Josie teased. "They can't help that they're slimy. You should see them underwater; they're beauties." She bent down and studied the goop. "This is a medusa jelly. They have a particularly sensitive digestive system. Poor guy probably ate something he shouldn't have. Probably litter or pollution."

I reached down and helped Dario up, and we continued toward the big event.

"Let's not mention this to anyone," he said after he'd composed himself enough to realize he'd overreacted.

"My lips are sealed," I said.

TJ was the first person I saw. He smiled and spread his arms wide.

"Welcome to the bonfire."

Fifteen

Stella

Bonfire
June 19 (Continued)

"I knew you'd make it," TJ said, mostly to me. Then he asked Dario and Josie, "Hey, guys, you want a marshmallow? There's a big bag of them over there. And sticks. Help yourself."

"I never say no to a marshmallow." Dario headed for the bag. "Browned on the outside and gooey on the inside. That's how I like 'em."

Josie followed him, saying, "You drink those smoothies to stay healthy, but then you eat toasted blobs?"

"They cancel each other out," Dario replied.

Suddenly out of nowhere, Apple was next to them. "I like 'em burned on the inside and burned on the outside." They were too far away for me to hear the rest.

"She has a point about smoothies and marshmallows," TJ said. He led me a few feet away from the fire and sat on a blanket. I followed him and did the same.

I was at a bonfire, sitting on a blanket on the beach, next to TJ. *This* was exactly what I hoped this summer would be like.

"How's your guard training going?" I asked.

"I don't want to brag, but I think I'm at the top of the pack."

"Oh yeah? What about Tucker and Timmy?" I asked.

"Tim's doing okay. Tuck needs to pick up his pace on the runs."

"What if he doesn't?"

"Technically, he won't be offered a job here next year, but we have an in with the mayor, so it shouldn't be a problem. In fact, we're expecting to complete the program early."

"How did you get to be friends with the mayor?" I asked

"He was watching us train one day and sort of introduced himself. He's a nice guy," he said. "They say it's all about who you know."

"That would be good for your five-year plan."

"You remember that?" he asked, surprised.

"Sure. Why wouldn't I?"

"I dunno." He shrugged. "I mean, *I* know everything going on in *your* life. You post on Instachat like ten times a day. But I don't do that."

Well, he didn't know *everything,* because, obviously, I only post the good stuff. "Come on," I said. "I saw that pic of you in the ugly Christmas sweater and your new dog and that bruise on your knee when you fell off the curb. So I know stuff. Plus, I have a good memory, and I just remember that you're always planning."

He looked at me; I could see the firelight flicker in his eyes. "You cold?"

I didn't realize that I was hugging my knees into my chest. "A little."

"Maybe we should move closer to the fire?" he asked.

"That's okay. I'm fine here." I wanted to be a little in the distance, where we could talk without yelling over the music, and as long as I had Apple in my sight, I didn't have to worry about her appearing on our blanket without warning. *That* would be awkward. I hoped Josie would mingle or at least talk to Timmy. Dario, on the other hand, was being very social among the marshmallow scene. He tossed one to Tucker, who tried to catch it in his mouth. Then Tucker threw one to Dario, only that one was melting, and it went everywhere but his mouth.

I shivered. TJ slid his red hoodie over his head and handed it to me. "Put this on."

I did. I acted casual about it, but inside I was like, *Wow!* because I'd always wanted to wear one of those. It was already warm from his body heat, and it smelled like a combo of sunscreen, deodorant, and fabric softener. I used to spend time like this with Pete, but when all of that fell apart, I seriously thought I'd never like a guy again.

He asked me, "Do you have big plans for the summer?"

"Not really," I said. "Except that I have to stay out of trouble. My mom put me on this three-strike thing, and let's just say I only have one left."

"What were the first two?" he asked. I would've asked too.

I took a deep breath.

"I made some new friends this year, and they go to the mall after school to hang out. I wanted to go, but I had track practice. So I told my coach that I had a bunch of doctor appointments, and I skipped practice."

I pause. "But the coach saw my mom and asked how I was feeling. My mom didn't know what Coach was talking about. And the next day the coach asked me to return my uniform."

He said, "That's pretty bad, but not terrible.

"I made it worse."

He waited for me to go on, but I wasn't ready to do that.

"Can we talk about something else?" I asked finally.

"Sure. So, no big plans for the summer?"

"Nah. This is vacation, so I'm just going to see what happens," I said. "Tomorrow we're gonna snorkel, so that's a one-day plan."

"Action-packed day." He laughed. "What else, like longer-term for the summer?"

I wasn't sure what he was getting at. I shrugged.

"Like, do you think about people you might hang out with?"

"Uh, I guess not. . . ."

"If you did think about that, would I be one of those people?" he asked.

Now I got what he was getting at. And I liked where he'd gotten.

"I hope so. I mean, I'd like to."

He smiled. "I was thinking we could do something together sometime. You like Skee-Ball?"

I felt my face flush. "I love it. I'm really good at it too."

A group of girl guards started singing and dancing to the latest Flying Fish song, "A Basket Full of Seashells." I sort of lip-synched along, and TJ's legs bobbed to the beat.

TJ asked, "Which band member is your favorite?"

Without thinking, I said, "Evan. You?"

"Hard to say. Depends on the song. Austin's drum solo in this one is great. But Lucien rules the keyboard in 'Sand on My Towel.'"

"I agree with both of those, but Evan is the best dancer."

"That's not fair. Since he's on the guitar, he can move around, and the other guys can't."

"True," I said.

"You like a guy who can dance?"

"Sure." I turn to him. "Do you dance?"

"Not even a little," he said. "I hope that's not a deal breaker."

"I can show you some moves."

"You're on."

I saw Josie move away from the crowd and head in our direction. She covered a yawn with her hand. "You ready, Stell?" she asked.

"Umm," I started. I was going to ask her if she wanted to stay for a while longer, when a four-wheeler tractor growled behind us. Timmy was driving.

TJ started putting on his Reefs.

He said, "Sorry to cut this short, but me and the guys have something we have to do." He stood and wiped the sand off his legs. "Tuck!" he called. "We gotta go."

Timmy left the four-wheeler running but got off to talk to Josie. "Hey," he said. "Sorry I didn't get here earlier. Do you want a lift back to the boards?"

She looked at the distance from the fire to the boardwalk. "It's not far. I can walk."

"Oh," he said. "Okay. Maybe next time."

"Sure. Maybe." Then she asked, "Where are you going?"

"Secret lifeguard meeting," Tim said.

He returned to the four-wheeler, where Tuck was already sitting, both cheeks plumped out with marshmallows and both hands full too. He couldn't talk, but he was able to pump up his muscular arms for us to see. It'd become his signature move.

TJ got on the tractor behind Tucker. He called to us, "See you guys tomorrow?"

"Yup," Dario managed to say, although some browned marshmallow dripped out the side of his mouth. He had white sticky marshmallow all over his face and hands. It was gross. I'm sure the Three *T*s had noticed.

The tractor roared away.

"Where's Apple?" I asked.

Dario made a *poof* motion with his marshmallow-coated hands.

I said to him, "Looks like you lost in the Great Marshmallow Battle." I was trying to drop a hint that he'd gone unnecessarily overboard with the marshmallows.

He checked out his hands, swallowed, and said, "Can one of you get my sandals?"

Josie bent down and looped her fingers in the straps; then she said to me, "Sorry about interrupting you guys."

Dario licked his fingers. "Interrupting what?" he asked. Then he looked at the guard sweatshirt I was still wearing. "Wait a minute. Were you having a *moment*? You and TJ? You like him? Is that what that was? A *moment*?"

"It wasn't a *moment*—" I started to explain, when Dario picked up his vibrating phone with his cleanest two fingers.

"Ugh. My mom. I gotta go before she puts out an APB on me." He ran on ahead of us. He wasn't kidding. He was late getting home one time last summer, and his mom called Officer Booth to their house. She wanted to file a missing-persons report and told Booth that he should have a helicopter out searching with a spotlight.

Josie's phone alarm went off. It was eight o'clock. This time I texted Dad to keep him in the loop. Dad wasn't the type to hover over us, as long as he knew we were safe.

Josie asked me, "What do you want to do now? I mean besides get something to eat? I can't believe there wasn't even a barbie there." She meant a barbecue.

I shrugged. "It's too early to go home."

She was quiet. Something was bothering her, and I was pretty sure I knew what it was.

"Don't worry about TJ. You and I are still going to do all the things we always do," I said. "But this year I also want to do some other stuff that we haven't done before."

"That's super, but that isn't what I was thinking about."

She went ahead without another word.

Sixteen

Stella

Police Station

June 25 (Continued)

I tell Santoro, because I have no one else I can talk to about this. "The bonfire was great. It was like things for my summer had turned around, and I was doing exactly what I'd wanted to do. And check this out." I turn to show him the back of the lifeguard sweatshirt. "But Josie . . ."

"What about her?" Santoro asks.

"It wasn't her scene. I wanted it to be, but it wasn't." I add, "She wasn't obvious about being bored, but I could tell. She didn't even try to talk to anyone other than Apple or Dario. And why couldn't she see that Timmy was crushing on her? And don't get me started with Dario and the marshmallows. It was . . ."

"What?"

"You're going to think I'm being mean again."

"I don't think you're mean," he says.

"That's good, because I'm not. I swear."

"So, what was Dario like?"

"Embarrassing."

"But Tucker was doing the same thing. From what you've said, it sounds like the two of them are a lot alike. But you don't think Tucker is embarrassing?"

"I never thought about that." Santoro is more perceptive than I gave him credit for. "Maybe."

He flips through his notebook to check a detail. "Where did TJ say they were going?"

"He didn't." TJ didn't tell me, so this isn't a lie.

Seventeen

Stella

Nifty Gifty

June 19 (Continued)

I was surprised when Josie said she didn't want to go home.

She suggested shopping, which was unlike her. She didn't have to ask me twice. I thought maybe she'd said it because she knew I was in the market for a new bathing suit, but when she told me what she wanted to buy, it all made sense.

We entered Nifty Gifty, which was crowded with out-of-towners going gaga over refrigerator magnets. Dario could trash talk about magnets all he wanted, but there was no denying they were a hot item.

I swiped through a rack of cute bikinis and pulled out a few that I liked.

Josie called to me from across the store, holding up a metal box. It looked like it would hold jewelry; bangle bracelets would fit in it really well. On top it said WHALEHEAD, NJ. It wasn't an exciting box, but it looked like it would do the job to replace our lost treasure box, so I shrugged. Then I held up a bathing suit, and Josie gave them a similar shrug, so I left it behind.

Josie paid for the box, and we met outside Nifty.

"It doesn't have a lock," she said. Our previous box was a little safe where people could put important papers, like passports, and it had a dial combination lock.

"That didn't help last time," I pointed out.

"True." Then she said, "Let's put it in our spot."

With our VIP bracelets, we cut in front of everyone in line at Kevin's Fun House, and when the coast was clear, we jumped through the hole in the floor to the sand below and pulled the trapdoor shut above us. Once again, we both landed on our butts.

"Where should we put it?" Josie asked. "Maybe we can hide it better?"

I looked around with the help of my phone's flashlight app. "We could bury it over there." I indicated a particularly dark area to the side of the new sliding door that blocked the sight of the ocean. "Or over there." I pointed to a spot at the edge of the Smoothie Factory's foundation. "Or over there." And I pointed to a spot near the foundation of Kevin's Fun House. "Not a ton of options."

She put her hands on her hips. "It's like you aren't even trying. Do you care about this at all?"

I did care about it, just not as much as Josie, but I knew that telling her that wouldn't go over so well. "I do, Jo. But there aren't many places to pick from, for real."

"You have a better idea?" she asked me.

"We could keep it at home. Then it wouldn't get lost again."

Josie just stared at me. Finally she said, "You can't be serious."

"What's the problem with that?"

"It's stupid. Boring." Then she raised her voice. "It breaks tradition!"

"Okay, okay. Let's bury it over there." I chose the spot by the Smoothie Factory's foundation, because there was a tuft of beach grass that must get enough sun poking through the boards to survive. "We can try to get it under the grass."

She nodded. Then she took the Flying Fish concert flyer out of her back pocket and put it into the box. "You have anything?"

I reached into my pocket for something, anything. I was unprepared for this, but, thankfully, I found something good. "Here's my ticket from my first Minotaur ride of the season."

"Good one." Josie smiled, and I was relieved that had made her happy. She crouched down and dug in the sand, placed the box in the hole, and covered it up. "Looks okay," she said.

The sliding door started to open, showing a nearly full moon hovering over the black waters of the Atlantic.

We looked at each other like, *What should we do?*

I bent into a shadow and tugged Josie to crouch next to me.

"Is that . . . ?" Josie started.

I shushed her and nodded.

The door slid open farther, and three kayaks were dragged through the sand, right along the groove. *That* explained the small trench in the sand.

They were lined up in a row against the wall of the Smoothie Factory, and one of the draggers knocked on the newly painted lime-green door. A girl in a white lab coat answered. "Hi, guys." Then she called behind her, "They're here!"

A second girl joined her at the door. I clearly saw their faces under the outside light, but I didn't know either of them.

The kayakers each lifted bags from their respective kayaks and handed them to the girls.

Josie whispered to me, "What's in the bags?"

I shushed her again.

One girl asked, "You want to come in and hang out?"

"Nah. We get up early." The kayakers dragged the boats through the groove in the sand out to Thirty-Fourth Street. We crept to a place where we could spy on them. There they hoisted the boats onto a trailer towed by a van and waved to the driver once all three kayaks were secure. One of the kayakers pulled a cell phone from the pocket of his shorts and thumbed a message; then he joined the other two, who were halfway up the ramp that led to the boardwalk.

My cell phone vibrated with a message from TJ. **Skee-Ball tomorrow?**

We inched out toward the street, still hidden in the darkness, and watched as the van rounded the corner onto the main street, Ocean Avenue. I noticed that it was a Water Sport Adventure van. The first person that popped into my mind was Angie, since she'd said she was driving one of their vans. I noticed something else that stood out. It was a person under a streetlight. They were particularly noticeable because they wore a Phillies baseball cap. Most people at Whalehead are Yankees or Mets fans, so a Phillies cap isn't popular.

"What do you think they were doing?" Josie asked.

"I don't know, but I want to find out."

"We can't really chase the van down Ocean Avenue," Josie said.

"No, we can't. We'll need to think of another way." I thought for a hot sec, and I couldn't come up with anything.

But Josie did.

Eighteen

Stella

Police Station

June 25 (Continued)

"You see the driver of the van?" Santoro asks.

"No." That isn't a lie. I assume it was Angie, but I don't know for sure.

"What about the people with the kayaks?"

"It was too dark." This time I lie, not because I'm a liar, although it might seem that way, but I know how this all unfolds, and none of those people are important to the conspiracy or the accident that brought me here in the first place. I know what it's like to get in trouble for something that isn't really your fault, and there's no reason the Three Ts or Angie need to be identified.

I ask, "Any word from the hospital?"

"Nothing yet." He adds, "I know you're worried, but no news is usually better than bad news."

I nod.

Santoro gets back to business. "What was Josie's idea? Her idea to find out what all this was about?"

"She suggested we ask about part-time jobs at the Smoothie Factory. You know, talk to the people who work there, specifically the girls at the basement door that night, and see what they were doing."

"Josie comes up with good ideas, huh?" he asks.

"Sure. But so do I, like with Meredith Maxwell," I say. "That was me."

Nineteen

Stella

Boardwalk—Whalehead, New Jersey
June 20

> "Murielle duPluie here with the Whalehead news from the Jersey Shore. If you're on the boardwalk today, you're going to want to stop in front of Kevin's Fun House, where the biggest welcome sign ever is being constructed for none other than Meredith Maxwell. The project is led by her self-proclaimed number one fan, Cassandra Winterhalter. This girl is determined to get as many signatures on the sign as possible, so swing on by."

"See ya," Josie called to Dad as we headed out for the day.

"We're going to put our names on the welcome sign," I added.

Dad said, "Hold it right there." He held out a ziplock bag of fresh-cut fruit for each of us. Then he kissed us each on the cheek, grabbed his tackle box, and headed out the door.

I asked, "No workout today?"

"I already did. I got a jump on the day while you two were sleeping." He added, "Don't forget sunscreen. By the way, we'll be having company for dinner tomorrow night."

"So soon?" Josie asked.

"You like her?" I asked.

"So soon?" Josie asked again.

"Girls!" He put his arms around both of us. "You are my number ones. Got it? It's just dinner."

"But—" Josie said.

"Seriously. We're just eating food at the same place. People do it all the time."

He hopped into his pickup truck and took off.

On our stroll to the boardwalk Josie asked, "It's soon, isn't it?"

"Maybe it really is just dinner." My phone vibrated.

It was a text from TJ. **So, Skee-Ball?**

"You too?" Josie asked me, somehow knowing that it was TJ.

"It's nothing," I told her when we came to a section of boardwalk covered with gulls.

An old man sat on a park bench feeding them his breakfast muffin. It sounds cute, but trust me, it isn't. The thing is, when you feed one seagull, others see, and they want to be fed too. And in no time, there's a swarm of birds aggressively pushing for a breakfast muffin. Not a crumb, the whole muffin. People hate when this happens, but the old man loved the attention. He directed them: "One at a time." "Don't be pushy." "Get to the back of the line." The gulls didn't follow the instructions.

We walked on the periphery of the muffin-eating flock.

In the distance we could see a crane setting up the new bungee ride on Murphy's Pier. There hadn't been a new attraction on the pier since the Minotaur was installed. There had been talk of a haunted mansion, but the city council chose bungee.

Josie popped a strawberry into her mouth. "So, first our Smoothie Factory inquiry and then snorkel, yeah?"

I went for a cantaloupe chunk. "Yup."

We stood in front of the Smoothie Factory. "What now?" Josie asked.

I said, "Let's go in and ask for an application."

Josie looked at the pack of people waiting in line, blocking the door. "How're we even gonna get inside?"

"We'll have to wait," I said.

"Ugh. I don't want anyone to see me in this line. If I'm going to boycott, it has to look like a boycott."

A girl in a white lab coat flattened herself between the

doorjamb and the crowd, and wiggled herself outside. Once free from the store, she removed her lab coat and name tag.

Josie and I looked at each other, each with the same idea. We followed for a few beats; then Josie nudged me to say something.

I said, "Um, excuse me."

The girl turned to see if I was talking to her. And as soon as I saw her face, I recognized her as the girl who had opened the basement door last night.

"Hi. Do you work at the Smoothie Factory?" I asked, but it was kind of obvious.

She twirled a band out of her hair and let it fall down. "Yeah."

"Well, we were wondering if you were hiring?" I asked.

Josie added, "Looks like you're super busy."

The girl looked at Josie, acting friendlier now. "I love your accent. Australian?"

"Yeah," Josie said. "Usually people guess British first."

"Well, you sound just like a man who's friends with the owners of the Smoothie Factory. He's in town for the week and at the store all the time. I love listening to him." Then she asked, "Maybe you know him?"

Josie said, "Uh, I don't know everyone in Australia, but maybe if I saw him, I'd recognize him."

"Wouldn't it be funny if you and him dock your boat at the same place or something?"

"So funny," Josie said.

The girl offered, "They're totally hiring. You interested? Because if you know that guy, you'd totally get the job."

"We're looking at our options," Josie said. "Do you like it there? How late do you work? Do you have to do stuff besides make smoothies, like make deliveries, or take deliveries, or do stuff in the basement?"

All of her questions made the girl pause. I explained, "She hates basements. Weird phobia."

The girl relaxed. "I like it. We work till about ten o'clock. And sometimes we take deliveries and clean the equipment. The cleaning isn't too bad, except for the big machine, which is in the basement, so you'd hate that. And it's a lot of work."

"What's the machine for?" I asked.

"Sorry." She giggled. "It's a secret that only certain Smoothie Factory employees know."

"For real?" I asked, as if the idea of a secret made me all sorts of excited. "Me and my sister are really good at keeping secrets."

"You're sisters?" She looked at me: dark hair and eyes, New Yorker. Then she looked at Josie: blond, blue-eyed, Aussie. "How is that possible?"

"Half sisters," Josie clarified.

The girl looked at me. "You drew the short straw on the accent, huh?"

I smiled at her rude comment only because I wanted to know the secret; if not for that, I probably would've shown her how loud a New York accent can get.

The girl laughed at her own joke and kept going. "Sorry, but unless you're inside the Smoothie Factory trust cocoon, I can't tell you that."

Trust cocoon?

She swiped her hair behind her ears. "I gotta go. But if you want, stop in and fill out an application. You can write down that I referred you. My name is Lydia." She picked up her pace, and that clearly ended our convo.

"Well, that wasn't helpful," I said.

"No, but she wasn't the sharpest swordfish in the school, if you know what I mean."

I did.

"We could try to intercept her again at this time tomorrow and tell her you were hired, and that I actually do know that Aussie mate, and get her to tell us the Smoothie Factory secret."

"Not a bad idea," I said.

On our way to pick up snorkel equipment from the Water Sport Adventure stand on the beach, I asked, "Secret machine in the basement?"

"Yeah. Do you think that's true, or is it some high-tech dishwasher, and she doesn't know it? Maybe her coworkers told her that the dishwasher, or whatever it is, is a big secret, to make cleaning it more exciting."

I laughed a little. "You might be right. A secret machine is way more interesting."

I'd gone snorkeling with Josie before, so I knew the drill. We put on masks and flippers. She swam under the pier, and I followed. Swimming with flippers is so much easier than without.

I didn't really know what we were looking for—heck, half the time I wasn't sure what I was looking *at*. I was surprised and sad to see trash down there: bottles, a tire, a chair. It felt like humans had invaded a world they didn't belong in. Talk about careless and lazy. Why throw a bottle into the ocean when we can recycle it?

While I assessed human disregard for the ocean, Josie investigated other things. And she made two interesting discoveries.

Twenty
Stella

Police Station
June 25 (Continued)

Santoro picks up his pen and asks, "What kind of discoveries?"

"We've snorkeled under the pier lots of times, so we know what it looks like. The pier is held up by wooden pylons, which are like telephone poles cemented into the ground. The pylons are coated with something to protect them. I don't know what it is, but it looks like wax. Well, Josie noticed that the pylons closest to the shore had less wax. It looked like some of it had been eaten away."

He writes that down. "How could you tell?"

"The wax shines, and the pylons closer to the shore were less shiny. Josie thought maybe fish had been nibbling at it. She had a big explanation like some species had lost its food supply,

maybe because of pollution, and that's why it was snacking on the pylon wax."

He isn't looking at me, because he's writing. "She sounds really smart about this aquatic stuff."

"She is, but in this case her theory was wrong. The wax had nothing to do with starving fish."

Twenty-One
Stella

603 Whalehead Street, Whalehead, New Jersey
June 21

"Murielle duPluie from WLEO here with the Whalehead news from the Jersey Shore. What a beautiful evening!

"As you know, I pride myself on being a thorough reporter. And I wouldn't be doing my job if I didn't give you some history about our celebrity guest. In my research I unearthed some lesser-known factoids about Miss Maxwell. As we know, she's all about health and fitness, but she hasn't always been this way. In fact, in 2016 she canceled concerts because she was sick and exhausted. But she doesn't get that way anymore. That's why she's coming to visit our very own Smoothie Factory to tell her story about how the nutrition-packed drinks changed her life."

Dad lifted tuna steaks off the grill and set the platter of fish on the patio picnic table. His new friend Laney shut the French doors and delivered to the table a colorful salad that included raspberries and pecans.

"Did you hear that?" Dad said about the report on WLEO. "Meredith Maxwell is a health nut too."

I passed the fish platter to Laney and in the process knocked her cell phone to the ground.

"Ohmigod," I said. "I'm so sorry. That was my bad." I bent down to get it for her, but her hand snatched it up. I mean, fast. She was on it like a viperous snake snapping up a field mouse. Very weird.

"I got it." Without looking at it, she said, "It's fine." She slid it into her pocket and went back to the fish platter.

"It could be cracked," I said. I wasn't sure, because I didn't know her, but I thought she was mad. "I'll totally pay for it," I offered.

She stopped serving fish and looked at me with a smile that I knew was fake. If she were in New York, the next words out of her mouth would have been, *Just shut up*. But she said, "It's just a phone," in a tone that didn't match the forced smile.

Josie and Dad hadn't noticed the look she'd given me, because Josie scooped salad onto my plate and hers. "Are you?" Josie asked Laney. "Are you a health-food nut?"

Laney left the phone subject behind and said, "I'm a vegetarian and work out, but I'm not gonna lie—I like my cotton candy."

Josie asked her, "What do you think of the Smoothie Factory?"

"I haven't tried it. I'm kind of loyal to the old Water Ice World."

"Thank you," Josie said. "That's what I've been saying all along."

"Plus," Laney added, "I would never wait in a line like that for anything."

"You and me both," Dad said.

"But you don't mind waiting for a fish to bite," I said to him.

"That's completely different!" He wiped his mouth. "So, the really big question is this, Laney," he started asking, "and this is important to see if you fit in around here. What piece do you usually use in Monopoly?"

This was something super important to get on the table before dating got serious. Me, Josie, and Dad always used the same ones. Josie was the shoe, Dad was the hat, and I was the race car. If Laney chose one of those, this match was doomed.

Laney said, "This is a lot of pressure. I don't want to say the wrong thing. But I'm pretty committed to . . ."

We all stopped eating to listen to her answer.

"The thimble!" she declared.

"Phew," Dad said. "You can stay."

"I'm so glad," she said. The rest of the dinner, Laney was funny and relaxed, which was totally the opposite of the glimpse of the woman I had seen when I'd reached to pick up her phone. But the real test of whether she would be able to hang with the Higleys would be in Monopoly, because we don't mess around.

Me and Josie cleaned up dinner while Dad and Laney set up the game. When Josie and I were in the kitchen alone, I said, "I don't know about her."

She looked outside at Laney and Dad. "I didn't like this whole idea, but she seems like she could be great for Dad."

"Did you see the phone thing earlier?" I asked.

Josie just shrugged. "She knew it was an accident."

I shook my head. "That was fake. She never even checked it to see if it was fine. She just didn't want me to see it."

"Why?"

I said, "She's hiding something."

Dad joined us and whispered, "You like her?"

"She's super," Josie said.

I smiled, but didn't actually answer.

Dad grabbed a bowl of pita chips. "Let's see how she navigates the board—you know, how she handles going straight to jail without passing Go."

Laney bought every property she landed on, and before long me, Dad, and Josie were all bankrupt. We had a lot of laughs, but I watched her very carefully for any hint that there might actually be a snake under that exterior. I didn't see anything suspicious, but I really wanted to get my hands on that phone.

"This is one for the books," Josie said.

"I'll say," Dad said as he slid the paper money back into the box. "A real estate tycoon, you are."

Josie got up from the table. "Can you handle the cleanup while we go to the arcade?"

"Sure thing." He added, "Be home by ten."

I looked at my watch, crinkled my forehead, and then looked at Dad. "We're not in eighth grade anymore," I pointed out. "I think our curfew should reflect that."

He looked from me to Josie. "Thirty. Ten thirty."

Josie considered this a victory, but I wasn't done negotiating.

I crossed my arms in front of my chest.

"Fine. I give up," he said. "Ten forty-five and not a minute later."

"Deal," I said.

"Wait." He waved me over. "Stay out of trouble." He kissed the top of my head. Then he told Laney, "Those two." He held up his finger. "They got me wrapped around it."

She said, "They're great girls."

I paused at the door and watched Dad turn on the TV,

then go into the kitchen to make coffee. Laney sat on the couch, slipped the phone out of her back pocket, poked in a password, and swiped her finger around the screen as she scanned it. Then she set it on the end table.

"Josie, wait," I said. "I need to get a peek at her phone."

She rolled her eyes. "For real?"

"It'll only take a minute." I added, "Hurry, before the password locks.

"Fine." Josie stepped back into the living room. "Hey, Laney, can I talk to you for just a minute?"

"Okay." Laney followed Josie onto the back porch.

I heard Josie say, "Here's the thing about my dad . . ."

I looked at the phone. No crack. *Phew*. Then I swiped through her camera roll. There were pictures of boats.

Boat, boat, boat.

Actually one boat. Lots of pictures of the same one. There was a cropped photo of its name, the *Koala*.

I was just about to put the phone down when I flicked to a photo of a man. And I swiped through shot after shot of this guy. He wasn't posing; he didn't look like he knew his picture was being taken. I really quickly took out my phone and snapped a picture of the man. *She's dating my dad and has all these pics of some other guy?*

I put her phone back as Josie and Laney returned.

Laney said, "You girls are so sweet to worry about your dad."

I smiled at her, and I promise that my fake smile was

more believable than Laney's. "Thanks for understanding," I said, even though I didn't know what Josie had been talking about.

Josie said, "Let's get going."

We left.

"So?" Josie asked.

"I was right." I told her about the pictures.

"That doesn't mean anything."

"Maybe."

Suddenly Josie started racing.

"Or maybe it does," I said to myself.

I knew I couldn't keep up, and I didn't try. I didn't want to wipe out in these gladiator sandals, plus this denim skirt wasn't really made for a marathon. I had managed to talk Josie into a more stylish outfit—I loaned her a cute tank top, cropped leggings, and Chucks—and it was still comfortable enough for her to race a spontaneous 5K.

"I give up," I said.

"Stell, let's start jogging tomorrow, okay?"

"Why?"

"Because you should be able to zip to the arcade without losing your breath!"

"Nah," I said.

"Well, I didn't want to go to a bonfire, but I did."

"Touché," I conceded. "Fine."

Twenty-Two

Arcade

June 21 (Continued)

Dario was already at the Skee-Ball section of the arcade. "Ever notice that some of the lanes mysteriously acquire more balls than others? Don't worry. I fixed it. They each have seven."

"I'm gonna get popcorn," I said. "Anyone want anything?"

"No. But you gotta do me a favor," he said.

"What?" Josie asked. "I'll do it while Stell gets the popcorn."

"You have to go in the bathroom and wash your hands."

"They aren't dirty," she said.

He held one hand in front of my nose and the other in front of Josie's. "Smell."

We did.

"This place has incredible soap. I'm dying to know if it's the same in the girls' room. This is a news story in the making. A comparison of soap up and down the boardwalk. And right now, I gotta tell you, this place is in the lead." He smelled his hands again.

Josie said, "I'll admit. That's some nice-smelling soap, but I don't know if the topic has news potential."

"Just do me a favor and check the soap," Dario said. "I know what's news."

I went for the popcorn and looked for TJ. Turned out that a red GUARD T-shirt was in front of me in line.

I cleared my throat, and TJ turned around and said, "Hey. You're late."

"We didn't say a time, and I had this tournament thing—"

"Tennis tournament?"

"No. Never mind," I said.

It was his turn to order. He said, "I'll have a Coke and"—he turned to me—"what do you want?"

"Popcorn," I said.

He bought it and gave it to me. Maybe in an effort to be cute, he bent his head over the bag and took a popped corn into his mouth. "Buttery and salty," he said. He'd succeeded, because it was cute.

"Popcorn usually is," I said. "Thanks for this." Then I asked, "You gonna play a few rounds with us?"

He looked at his watch. "Man, I'd love to, but I gotta go

and take care of something. How long will you be here? I could come back."

I resisted the urge to ask him about where he was going tonight. *Is it the same as last night? And why doesn't he tell me what he's doing?* "We have to be home at ten forty-five."

"Okay. Maybe I'll see you later."

"I don't know. It sounds like your social schedule is pretty full this summer," I said playfully.

"Are you *mad*? Is Stella Higley a little upset that I have other plans without her?" he teased back. "Are you starting to like me?"

"What? No. Don't go getting a big head. It's nothing like that."

"Oh, right," he said, but I don't know that he believed me. "Look, this thing I have to do . . . it's only for this week. It's a little side job that's important. It'll be over soon, and then . . . maybe we can hang out more?"

Then he leaned his head into the popcorn bag again, even though he had a free hand, and bit another corn. "Yum." He lifted his brows up and down. "Have fun, and if I don't see you tonight, come by the shack tomorrow."

I watched him leave the arcade. Before he was out of sight, he turned and mouthed to me, *I like you, too.*

I couldn't hold back a big smile.

It was so nice to know what he felt about me. I still kind of wished Pete had been like that. I was so mad at him, because it'd felt like he'd been lying to me, but he really never had, I guess.

I liked the idea of TJ hanging out with me for the rest of the summer. *But what's with this secret weeklong job?*

I rejoined Josie and Dario at the Skee-Ball machines. Dario had already wrapped himself in tickets like a mummy, and Josie had her hand in front of his nose.

"Looks like I missed all the fun." I held the popcorn out for them.

Josie said, "He was right about the soap."

I smelled her hand.

Dario said, "And I think something's wrong with this machine, because it's spitting out tickets like crazy. If I keep this up, I'll have enough for a Tootsie Roll *and* a piece of gum."

"Big score," I said. We had all agreed that playing Skee-Ball was more fun than the prizes. We'd grown out of prizes a long time ago.

I said to Josie, "We need to go back under the boardwalk."

She began to ask, "Wh—"

She stopped talking when she saw what Rodney was doing.

Twenty-Three

Police Station

June 25 (Continued)

Santoro stands up and walks around the table. He stretches one arm across his chest and pulls it with the other, then does the same with the other side. "What was Rodney up to?"

"It seemed crazy at the time," I say. "He was bent over studying the baseboards inside the arcade. He would crawl a little too. He said, 'It's coming from somewhere' and 'Where's it coming from?'"

"Did you ask about it?"

"I did. He said, 'The toxin.' He was looking for a toxin."

Twenty-Four

Stella

Boardwalk

June 22

> "Murielle duPluie from WLEO here with the Whalehead news from the Jersey Shore. The countdown has begun, thanks to Meredith Maxwell's number one fan, Cassandra Winterhalter. Stroll past the welcome sign in front of the Smoothie Factory to get a glimpse of the countdown to the Flying Fish concert, just five days away."

It looked like the kind of beach day you dreamed about: bright blue sky with only a slight puff of white clouds here and there. White sand sprinkled with people, beach umbrellas, and volleyball players. Unfortunately, it *felt* like the kind of beach day you dread—ninety-five degrees at nine in the morning and high humidity. I was sweating through my shirt before we started working out, and I think I felt the tops of my feet getting sunburned right through my shoes and socks. It was totally possible that my sneakers might melt right on the boardwalk. And there was no breeze at all. Fish were rotting somewhere, that was for sure; I could smell the funk.

I decided that when we went to the beach later, I would put my chair in the water and not move it all day.

But Josie had other ideas. She actually wanted to run in this weather.

I agreed to jog with Josie like we'd done lots of times before. The difference is that those other times I'd been part of the track team, and I'd wanted to be good at running. I wasn't on that team anymore, and, well, I was out of shape. I told her I'd go if she agreed we could go to the guard shack so that I could see TJ. "Timmy will probably be there," I said to Josie.

"Probably," she said, but no hint of noticing that he was a cute boy who'd been noticing her.

"So, I think he likes you," I said.

When she didn't answer, I added, "Do you like him?"

Still no answer.

"Josie?"

When she didn't answer the third time, I realized that

she was wearing earbuds and couldn't hear me. I gave up and stuck mine in too.

We ran past the old man feeding the seagulls again, and I got a splat of bird poop on my shoe. Gross.

We exchanged waves with Rodney, Kevin (the owner of Kevin's Fun House), Dario's mother, and other locals trying to enjoy what would be the coolest part of the day. That's what things are like at the shore—everyone is happy and friendly. It's the opposite of home, but I still love New York.

I saw Mayor Lopez talking to a woman I didn't know. I took out an earbud when I said hi.

He replied, "Hello, girls."

Before we got more than a few feet away, I leaned down to tie my shoe, which hadn't melted. With the earbud still out, I heard the woman say, "He's in the way."

Mayor Lopez said, "I can't just have him locked up for no reason."

"Then think of one," she growled, and marched with purpose toward the Smoothie Factory.

Twenty-Five

Police Station

June 25 (Continued)

"What was that all about?" Santoro asks.

"I wouldn't figure that out until later. At this point I didn't even know who this woman was, but she had great taste in shoes—spiky Jimmy Choos that looked glam with soft blue shorts and a flowy peasant top."

"Uh-huh."

"Do you want me to tell you more about the mayor and the lady now?"

"No. Let's stick to the timeline and just let me know what happened next."

Twenty-Six
Stella

Beach
June 22 (Continued)

I put the earbud back in, then caught up to Josie, who was already at the top of the ramp that led to the sand. We ran down the beach to the guard shack. Immediately I regretted suggesting the shack, because running on the sand was so much harder than the boards.

We found Timmy's legs dangling off the side of the raised hut. "If you're not careful, someone will recruit you for our training program," he said, more to Josie, who was ahead of me and was barely out of breath.

"Water?" I managed to choke out.

He handed me his bottle, and I gulped the water down.

Then I looked at Josie's outstretched hand. "Oops," I said, because I'd drunk it all.

Josie let out a huff. "Oh come on, Stell."

I said, "Sorry."

Timmy held out another drink for her, one in a lime-green cup.

She looked at it and shook her head. "You know I'm boycotting them."

"Okay." He sipped from the cup and smacked his lips. "Ahhh!"

She grabbed it. "Fine. This is only because I could die of dehydration and rot right here in the sand if I don't drink this. For the record, I want everyone here to know that I'm not ending my boycott. This is a life-or-death situation."

"Noted," Timmy said.

She wrinkled her forehead as she drank.

"What's wrong? Do you actually like it?" Timmy asked her.

"What type of smoothie is this?" she asked.

"Honeydew and mango. Why?"

She said, "There's something else in it. Something that I know, but I don't know, you know?"

"No," Timmy said, and he snatched the cup back.

I pointed to Tucker. "What's he doing?"

Tucker was on a stool with binoculars glued to his face, staring out at the ocean.

"He's spying."

"On what?" I asked.

"I'm not supposed to say," Timmy said. "It's a secret."

"Remind me never to tell you something secret," Josie said. "Because telling everyone you have a secret doesn't keep the secret. It makes people want to know more about the secret. See how that works?"

"Ah, right." Timmy pointed to her head. "You're smart."

I said, "But since you've slipped up this much, now you have to tell us. Spill it."

"No can do," he said. "I'll just say it's called the *Koala*, and that's it. Nothing else."

Josie pointed to herself. "I know koalas. They're Australian, you know."

"I do now," Timmy said.

I knew a *Koala* too. I asked, "What's so special about it that he's spying on it?"

"I'll just say that they're doing something, and that's it. Nothing else."

"What are they doing?" Josie asked.

"Dunno. That's why Tuck's spying. And it's a good thing I don't know, or I might accidentally tell you what I know. You know?"

"I know," Josie said. "It's not your fault. Secrets are hard for some people to keep."

Timmy smiled. "Thanks for not pressuring me, or I might've given something away."

"No problem," I said. "We're considerate like that." Then I called to Tucker. "Hey, can I look?"

He handed me the binoculars. "Just bird-watching," he said.

"Sure," I agreed, and focused the binoculars out to sea.

"Yup," I said. "I know that boat."

"How?" Josie asked.

"It's the one Laney had on her phone."

"Who's Laney?" Timmy asked.

"Dad's blind date from the other night," I said.

"That's so awkward," Timmy said. "Why don't they meet online like everyone else?"

"That would make more sense," I said.

"Hold up," Josie said. "You went into her pictures? I thought you were just checking if it was broken. That's such a violation of her privacy."

"Well, I did it, and I also found this." I showed them my photo of the man. "She had a lot of pictures of this guy. Like she's obsessed with him."

"How do you have that?" Josie asked.

"I took a picture of the picture on her phone with my phone."

"Not cool, Stell," Josie scolded. "It's probably like her brother, or uncle, or something."

Timmy joined in. "Or an old friend who died and she wants to remember him." He reached into a cooler and gave us each a cold bottle of water. "Come on. I'll give you a ride back up to the boards."

Timmy fired up the four-wheeler, and we got on behind him. Josie, then me.

"You can hold on," he said to Josie.

Sand flew up behind the back wheels as he drove us to the boardwalk. Little kids stopped their castle building to look at us. I imagined they were thinking we were the cool older girls getting a four-wheeler ride from a lifeguard (in training).

Before Timmy pulled away from the edge of the boardwalk, he reached down, picked a small shell out of the sand, and gave it to Josie. "Here," he said. "This is very special to me. Watch it until I get off work, will you?" He sped away before Josie could object.

Twenty-Seven

Stella

Police Station

June 25 (Continued)

"What was so important about that shell?" Santoro asks.

He doesn't get it.

"Nothing. Timmy was just being flirty."

"Giving Josie a plain old shell was flirting?"

"Yeah. It was cute."

He raises his eyebrows. "If you say so."

I ask him, "Do you have a wife or girlfriend?"

He pulls an elbow behind his head to stretch his arms instead of answering me.

"You're not gonna tell me? I'm telling you so much stuff."

"None of this is about me." His refusal to answer me gives me my answer—no wife, no girlfriend.

"Guess what she wanted to do with that shell."

Twenty-Eight

Stella

Boardwalk

June 22 (Continued)

I started toward home, dying for a shower, but Josie dawdled near Kevin's Fun House.

"Whatcha doing?" I asked.

"I want to put this in the box." She held up the shell.

"Now?"

She nodded.

On our way I asked her, "Do you like him?"

She shrugged. "Maybe. I don't know. I never liked a guy before."

"Well, if it helps, the fact that you want to save that shell in the box tells me you like him, too. At least a little."

"You know so much about this stuff. I mean, you had

Peter, and I feel like I'm behind schedule or something. It's embarrassing."

So I may have led Josie to believe that Pete and I were more than just friends. It didn't feel like a lie, because I'd believed it myself. The problem, as I learned the hard way, was that he never thought that.

Josie added, "At home you have boyfriends, and, just like that, TJ likes you now. It's like I can never catch up to you. And I don't like it."

I couldn't believe what I was hearing. "I'm sorry, Josie. I didn't mean to make you feel that way. And, for the record, I don't."

"Don't what?"

"Date and have boyfriends."

"You don't? But Pete— And I mean, look at you, acting all high school already."

I knew she didn't mean it as a compliment, but I liked that I acted high school. That was what I was going for. "Josie, don't laugh—"

"About what?"

I stopped walking and went over to the boardwalk's wooden railing. "When I tell you that I've never kissed a boy."

"But I thought—Peter?"

"We were really good friends, maybe even best friends, for a long time, like years, hung out all the time and studied together. We had a streak over six hundred days."

"That all sounds good," Josie said. "Perfect boyfriend."

"Correction: a boy who was my friend. Not boyfriend. I thought it was more than it was. It's embarrassing." I used my dirty shirt to wipe sweat off my top lip, then cracked open the bottle Timmy had given me, drank a big gulp, and rolled it on my forehead. "So don't be hard on yourself."

"What happened with Peter?"

"He told me he liked Kelsey Gelfman, the popular girl in school. To make it worse, he told me he'd liked her *forever*. And I'd thought we shared everything. He had this whole crush going on, and he'd never told me about it."

"Did you ever tell him about your crush?" Josie asked. "On him."

"I didn't think I had to. I thought . . . he liked me back." I paused for a beat before adding, "And the timing of all this was so bad, because it was right when Mom and Gregory told me they were getting married, and I assumed Pete was going to be my date for the wedding, but I went alone. And I had to deal with all this mushy love right in my face."

"I'm sorry, Stella. What did you do?"

"For starters, I stopped talking to him!" I added, "And I cried a lot. I realized that he was pretty much my only friend. So I had to find friends."

Josie made some comforting noises. "The girls you went shopping with when you cut track?"

I asked, "You know about that?"

"Strike one? Yeah. But I don't know about strike two."

"It was dumb. So dumb." I sighed. I couldn't believe I was about to say all this out loud for the first time. "Those new friends? I told them about Pete and Kelsey. . . ."

"What did they do?"

"They took pictures of them and then altered them with a photo program and made the pictures . . . well, made them really terrible, and then they posted them online. Everyone saw. Pete and Kelsey were totally humiliated. And, of course, they thought I was behind it."

"But you weren't?"

"No." Then I added, "I was mad at Pete, totally mad. Kelsey, too, and she didn't even have anything to do with it. But who does that? That's just so mean."

With that, Josie took my hand and led us to the fun house line, which we didn't have to wait in. "Anyone who knows you knows you're not mean. Anyone who knows you knows you're awesome. And Pete missed out."

I smiled. "You know, Josie, you're so nice. You say the nicest things. Maybe if I'd been nicer and said nice things, it would've been easier to make friends."

"Trust me, you're nice," she said. That was so Josie—my ally, always. I thought that maybe I should make sure I had her back as much as she had mine.

Josie took my hand again and pulled me into the hall of

mirrors. We wiggled through the foam pillars, scaled the rope bridge, and were at the floorboards.

A hot sec later we dropped to the sand under the boardwalk. Josie tucked the shell away while I went over to the Smoothie Factory's freshly painted basement door that we'd gone through many times before. "I wonder if the bags are in here. We could see what's in them. I'm dying to know what those guys are up to that's so hush-hush." I didn't give her a chance to respond. "Only one way to find out." I turned the knob, but sure enough it was locked. "Darn. I thought we could check out that secret machine, too."

Then there was a sound from the other side of the door, and it cracked open.

"Go! Go!" I pushed Josie into the shadows away from the door. We crouched down.

Lydia, the girl who we'd asked about jobs, stepped out, tossed a bag of trash into a can, and went back in.

The lock didn't catch.

Twenty-Nine

Police Station
June 25–26

I tell Santoro, "So I stuck my hand in the door to hold it open, and I led Josie inside."

"You entered the premises?"

"Yeah."

He rubs his hands over his face. "Geez." Then he stands up and bends at the waist, wincing. "Let's take a break right there. I'm going to go talk to Josie for a while.

"Your dad called your lawyer. Is it Greg?"

"Gregory," I correct with sort of an eye roll.

"You don't like him?" he asks.

"I do."

He gives me a look. "You know, he's driving all the way down here in the middle of the night."

"I know. He's fine. In fact, when I got in trouble at school, he's the one who came up with the three-strikes thing. It calmed my mom down."

"So he wanted to give you more chances." Then he asks, "Kind of ironic, isn't it?"

"What is?"

"That he came up with a system to give you more chances, and it sounds like you aren't giving him one."

I pause for longer than a hot sec. "That's a fair thought, Detective," I finally say.

"Let's bring your dad in." He waves at the window.

Dad opens the door. "How's it going?"

"She's doing great," Santoro says. "She has a lot to say. Lots of details."

Dad looks at me. "You okay?"

"I'm fine."

Santoro looks at his watch. "It's just after midnight, and I'd like to talk to Josie. Stella can stretch her legs or whatever."

"Thanks, Jay," Dad says to him.

"No problem. But do me a favor. There's a lot of context that I wouldn't want to get lost, so don't talk to anyone else about this except your lawyer. Do you know if he's almost here?"

"Yeah. Should arrive soon." Dad asks, "Any word from the hospital?"

"I got a text a little while ago," Santoro says. "It's touch and go."

We get to the hallway, and I realize how hot it's gotten in that little room, and how loud it is out here. People are in line to talk to the front desk sergeant; police radios and scanners chirp, bleep, and chatter with instructions from operators; and uniformed officers on breaks laugh about "You won't believe what this guy did . . ."

I look in a window to another interview room, where a detective is screaming at some guy handcuffed to a table. I mean, right in his face. I wonder if Santoro does that. He probably does. The guy thrashes around; it must hurt his wrists, and create those nicks and dents that I saw in the table. I'm dying to know what this guy did.

Santoro walks away, but I call him back. "Detective?"

He turns. "Yeah, Stella?"

I step up to him and realize how tall he is.

"Can you take it easy on her?"

He says, "You might not believe this, but I'm a nice guy. I'm only interested in finding out how that girl ended up in the hospital."

"It's just that, you know, I'm from New York, so I can handle all this"—I indicate the police station—"a little better than Josie." I add, "She scares easy."

"Got it." He goes to walk away again.

"One more thing," I say.

He turns around to listen, but he twists his neck to give it a crack, and I think that's a sign that I'm frustrating him.

"It was me. I held the basement door open, and I dragged Josie inside to look around."

Part Two

Josie

Thirty

Police Station
June 26 (Continued)

Detective Santoro is a good listener. He takes some notes to help him remember stuff. It's thoughtful of him to give me a Coke and chips. It must be late, because I'm getting really tired. I wonder if he has kids, maybe a daughter. He doesn't smile much. I think maybe he's so used to trying to be scary that he forgot how not to. And he is . . . scary, that is. I'd prefer it if he'd smile. I wonder how Stella is. I hope she's okay. She's had a rough year; she doesn't really need this drama.

"How did this all make me feel?" I ask myself, because I figure that would be the detective's next question. "I was really happy that we were both excited to find out what was going on in Whalehead—the pier, the Three Ts' secret trips under the boardwalk, the machine in the Smoothie Factory basement."

Detective Santoro pushes a corner of his lip up, but it looks like it takes great effort for him to do it.

"I felt good that Stella and I shared an interest in this adventure."

"That's nice. Thanks for sharing," Detective Santoro says. "But can we talk about things that happened? You know, the facts."

"I guess I wanted you to have the whole picture," I say. "Just before the basement door closed, I stuck my hand in it. To hold it open. Then we froze there for three winks. When it seemed like the girl wasn't coming back, I pushed the door open and peeked inside. No one was there, so I said to Stella, 'Let's go in and look around.'"

Detective Santoro closes his flippy notebook, leans back in his chair far enough that the front legs lift, and rocks a bit. He stares at me like I've confused him.

I clarify. "Stella didn't want to go inside, but I told her she was a wimp if she didn't."

He raises his eyebrows a little at that. "It was your idea to go inside?"

"Right. All me."

"And you told Stella that she was a wimp if she didn't?"

"That's right."

"I talk to a lot of people; I can usually spot the troublemakers. And you don't seem like the type to sneak into a place," he says.

"Sneaking? No. We've gone in through that door hundreds of times. We just wanted to look around. It wasn't really sneaking."

Thirty-One

Josie

Under the Boardwalk

June 22 (Continued)

We'd been in this basement lots of times when it was Water Ice World, because it's easier to get back to the boardwalk by cutting through the store, rather than walking out to Thirty-Fourth Street and going around. Plus it was just more fun to take a shortcut. And sometimes Yasmina would give us free water ice.

While lots had changed upstairs in the main section of the store, the basement looked pretty much the same as when it had been Water Ice World. Lots of boxes, piles of cups, lids, and cleaning supplies. Except for one thing: A big machine was in the middle of the space, just like Lydia had mentioned.

The contraption hissed and squirted water out its bottom. The drainage flowed into a hole in the basement floor, in order to prevent flooding.

"What is it?" I asked Stella.

"It ain't a dishwasher." She looked at the drain in the cement floor. "Where d'ya think that goes?"

I said, "Same place all the local runoff goes—" Just as I was about to give her specifics, we heard voices headed our way from upstairs.

Stella tugged me by the sleeve to follow her behind a cardboard mountain, and she put a finger to her mouth, signaling me to be quiet.

It was Lydia and an older woman who I recognized, because Stella and I had seen her talking with Mayor Lopez when we were jogging. Actually, they hadn't been talking—she'd been yelling at him.

Lydia said, "It's going to be the highlight of the summer, Mrs. Gardiner. I can't believe you were able to arrange it."

There was the sound of the walk-in refrigerator opening as the woman, Mrs. Gardiner, said, "A promotional event with Meredith Maxwell is going to put the Smoothie Factory on the map. And that map covers the whole country."

"Will she actually come here?" Lydia's voice dipped as she entered the refrigerator. "Like, can I meet her? A photo op?"

I had to struggle to hear the rest. "As long as it's okay with her people. She probably has to be careful. She has security and all," the woman, who I'd now pegged as the manager, or more likely the owner, said. Then she directed Lydia: "Just a few scoops. We don't have an endless supply."

Lydia asked, "Where do you get this—"

My cell phone vibrated with my alarm reminder to text Dad.

Stella's eyes popped out of her head at the hum of the phone.

I snagged it before Mrs. Gardiner and Lydia came out of the refrigerator, and texted Dad that we were at the Smoothie Factory, which I didn't like saying, because it implied I was actually buying something from there, and I didn't want him to think I'd broken my boycott.

Mrs. Gardiner was saying, " . . . brings it, but just once a year. So we have to make it last."

"How come no one else uses it, if it's so great, so healthy?"

"If I tell you, then it wouldn't be a secret ingredient," Mrs. Gardiner said.

"Okay, okay, but just tell me Meredith's schedule."

"She's coming to Whalehead, and she'll bop around the boardwalk for a bit, and then she'll come here for a smoothie and interviews with the news media. We're going to set up a cart on the boardwalk that day to be able to handle all the customers. We'll sell a million smoothies, which will make our investors very happy." Their voices muffled as they went back up the stairs. The last thing I was able to hear was "And after that, with her endorsement, there's no telling how big this business can get."

Once we couldn't hear them anymore, we slunk out from our hiding place, and I walked around the machine, studying it. That drain. It was a piece of the puzzle. When I snapped it in place in my brain alongside the clues I'd found while snorkeling, it started to form a picture. One I didn't like.

Stella said, "That Mrs. Gardiner lady is right. They'll sell a ton that day and forever with Meredith Maxwell's endorsement."

I didn't answer. Actually, I hardly heard Stella, because I was thinking so hard.

"We need to talk to Mr. Rodney," I said.

"About what?" Stella asked.

"What he was looking for in the arcade." I added, "The toxin. I think he was right."

Thirty-Two

Josie

Boardwalk

June 23

"Murielle duPluie here with all the shore news from WLEO. Finally the new bungee jump is installed on the pier, and wow is that thing high! Don't know if I'll have the nerve to try it.

"In other news, local experts have noted that Whalehead has an influx of dead jellyfish, a variety called medusas. They've been washing up onshore, so watch your step."

It had rained during the night, bringing with it much appreciated cooler air.

We set out for Mr. Rodney's bungalow via the boardwalk, dodging morning walkers, joggers, and Rollerbladers. It sounds safer than it was.

"Why are we going to see Mr. Rodney, aside from the usual entertainment value?" Stella asked.

"I want to learn more about this alleged toxin he was looking for in the arcade. It sounded crazy at the time, but now I'm not so sure."

"Sounds like a plan," Stella said while texting, I assumed with TJ.

I glanced out at the ocean. As a kid I hated going to the beach in the morning to find that my castle project from the day before had been leveled, but now I loved how when the tide came in at night, it smoothed the sand. It set up for a new day of fun and adventure on the beach.

"Ohmigod!" Stella grabbed me by the arm and twisted me around, turning my back to oncoming "traffic."

"What is it?" I asked.

"Something you don't want to see. For real. Trust me on this, Josie. Don't look."

After a comment like that, I had no choice. I turned and I saw it. It was our dad, Gary Higley. Rollerblading. Badly. Shirtless, knee-padded, elbow-padded, helmeted, holding Laney's hand. And, get this—her pads matched his! They were smiling and so focused on not falling or crashing that they didn't notice us.

"Phew," Stella said. "I thought that if they saw us, they'd stop to talk." She pinched her eyes shut incredibly tightly and reopened them.

"What are you doing?"

"Trying to unsee that." She blinked hard again. "It isn't working."

"Oh come on. They're wicked cute," I said.

"*Too* cute," Stella said. "Besides, I don't trust that lady."

I asked, "How can you not trust a lady who rollerblades with matchy-matchy safety pads?"

"Whatever is going on with the *Koala,* the boys' nightly escapes on kayaks to deliver something from the boat to the Smoothie Factory—she's somehow involved. Why else would she have so many pics of the boat? And that guy, the man. I think she's leading a double life."

"Why would Dad's friend set him up with someone living a double life?" I asked.

She said, "Maybe he didn't know. It's a *secret* double life."

"But that fishing buddy is a detective, so he'd know."

"Maybe," Stella said, "he's not a very good detective."

Thirty-Three

Josie

Police Station

June 26 (Continued)

Detective Santoro looks up from his flippy pad. "What was that?"

"Sorry. That was before she met you. She probably has a different opinion now."

"My feelings don't get hurt easily," he says. "I'm tough."

"Of course you are. You probably have a tattoo, right?"

He rubs his eyes like he has some kind of headache.

"Do you get migraines? Sometimes that's from not drinking enough water, you know."

"Josie, it's late. All this is very helpful information, but let's try to stay on track? Okay?"

"For sure, Detective Santoro," I say. "You got it."

Thirty-Four

Josie

Boardwalk

June 23 (Continued)

Dario's sister, Angie, called from behind us, "Was that your dad?"

"Yeah," I said.

"Nope," Stella said.

Angie Imani laughed. "Hey, I have parents too, so I totally get it. Mine are more embarrassing, by the way. I just hope your dad and his lady friend don't take out a trash can or something. You know, cause a scene and end up in a viral video."

"Geez. Let's hope that doesn't happen," Stella said.

Angie was so pretty. A lanyard crowded with keys and her Water Sport Adventure ID badge dangled from her neck, and she held her phone in a totally cute seashell case in one hand, and held a lime-green smoothie cup in the other. A Coach wristlet hung under the cup. She could've put everything in a purse or backpack, but the way she had it made her hands look dressed-up and busy. She was like an important woman on the move.

"Whatcha up to today?" Stella asked Angie. Stella'd been dying to hang out with her forever, but Angie never had an interest. Stella thought it was because Angie was older than us, which makes sense, but I think it's more because she always thought of us as her nerdy little brother's mates, and there was a rule somewhere that said she couldn't be friends with Dario's mates.

"You know, living the dream," Angie said. "I work at WSA at ten, grab lunch at Sprouts with Trish, and I'm moonlighting to earn a little extra moolah. Can you believe my dad is making me pay for my own insurance this year?" She wrapped her perfectly glossed lips around the wide straw.

"Moonlighting?" Stella asked. "What's that?"

"An extra night job. Just for a few days—actually, nights. It's cool."

Stella said, "Sounds cool."

I studied the cup that was clearly from the Smoothie Factory, but instead of saying "Whalehead, NJ" under the logo, it said SHELTER HARBOR, NJ. I pointed to it. "I didn't know they had a store there."

"Oh yeah. It's perfect for me. I get a breakfast smoothie

down there when I pick up the van, and then later in the day, I get a second one up here." She jutted out her chin. "Can you even believe how awesome it's making my skin?"

Her skin *did* look fab.

"I can't believe the vitamins in these things. You can look up all the values online. It's off the hook. I could eat spinach all day and not get this much iron." She held out the cup, indicating that was the source of the iron. "It's totally worth waiting in line, if you ask me."

I said, "I miss Water Ice World, personally."

"Oh, that was all sugar." Angie pointed a blue-polished fingernail at us; her lanyard jingled when she moved. "You guys should really incorporate these into your beach diet. You'll go back to school in the fall refreshed and radiant." She sipped again. "Sadly, Josie, I don't think Australia is in Mrs. Gardiner's expansion plans. But," she said to Stella, "New York is for sure."

"Expansion?" Stella asked.

"Yeah. If you become friends with Mrs. Gardiner, she might be able to hook you up with a job there," Angie said. "Business is booming. She wants to open more stores as fast as she can. She's got the investment and everything. Now she just needs to make it happen. I'm going to help her open the Bergen County store when the Water Sport Adventure season is over."

"Well, this store is hiring," I said.

"Don't I know it, but I can earn more tips at a store inland that's busy all year round." She flipped her wrist, accoutrements clanking together, and looked at her watch. "I gotta go."

"Okay. Catch you later," I said.

"Oh, I love that accent, Josie," Angie said.

"Hey," Stella jumped in. "Maybe we can check out the new bungee later tonight. You know, when you're done with your other thing, the moonlighting?"

"Looks fun. You totally should. Invite my brother. He'll hate it; he's so afraid of heights. And get a pic—I'll totally post one of him freaking out. Try to get him to puke, please. I'd love that," Angie said, and walked away with the sound effects of her embellishments banging together.

"You wanna bungee tonight?" Stella asked me, like I wouldn't notice that she'd really wanted Angie to go, and Angie had blown her off.

"Sure," I said.

Again, we made our way through the vacationers burning calories before the midday heat set in.

Folks exercised to a backdrop of organ music from the merry-go-round. Midway workers hosed last night's crumbs off the boards and into the water. I kept thinking about what Angie'd said. "How do you think Angie knows so much about the Smoothie Factory's expansion plans?"

"Sounds like she knows Mrs. Gardiner," Stella said while reading a text.

"She already has a job lined up at a store that hasn't even opened. How'd she manage that?" I asked. "Do you think maybe she's mates with that girl Lydia or someone else that works there?"

"Maybe," Stella said, again not really paying attention to me, instead focusing on her phone. "That would make sense." Things were quiet for a bit while she texted. When she was done, she looked up and asked, "Ready for the bungalow?"

Thirty-Five

Josie

Mr. Rodney's Bungalow

June 23 (Continued)

Mr. Rodney's bungalow wasn't much to look at. I'd imagined a bungalow made of bamboo and a thatched roof, like the type of hut you'd find on a Caribbean island nestled under a palm tree. But this was a small, one-story, one-bedroom house that was chockers of stuff needing attention: peeling paint, duct tape over a broken window, and weeds that had assumed control of the driveway that had once been ruled by gravel.

We went to the door, and I mentally added a broken doorbell to the list of needed repairs.

After a few rounds of knocking and calling inside through the cracked window, we decided Mr. Rodney wasn't home, or he was too asleep to hear us, or he just didn't want to answer the door.

"At home, grommets like to catch the waves early," I suggested. (Grommets are Aussie surfers.)

"Yeah. He's probably in the water," Stella agreed without looking up from her phone. She hadn't stopped texting since we'd left Angie.

"Stella?"

"What?" she asked with her eyes still down.

"Stella, can you put that down? We're doing something here."

Her arm dropped to her side with drama, followed by a sigh. "I'm making plans for tonight," she said.

"I don't care. It's super rude when you text like that when you're with someone. I mean, we're having a convo."

"Fine," she snapped, because "fine" usually ends an argument, right? "Well, we do have plans now."

Oh great, probably another bonfire where she could wear some more of TJ's clothes.

"Bungee," she said.

"Is it like a date for you and TJ? Because I don't want to go on your date."

She tilted her head and smiled. "No, not like a date. All three *T*s will be there, and Dario." She added, "Dario's not jumping."

I didn't answer, but my anger eased a little when I heard that Timmy would be there. I didn't want to admit it, but I was happy that she'd probably arranged that for me.

Thirty-Six

Boardwalk
June 23 (Continued)

Stella pulled some bangs out of my ponytail while we waited at the end of the pier.

"It's fine the way it is," I said.

"A little side bang is so in."

"I don't care," I said.

"I don't get that," Stella said with just a hint of anger, like she was frustrated that I wasn't more excited to look better, different, older.

"Why can't you let me look the way I look? You know, I don't look bad," I told her.

"Are you kidding? I didn't say you look bad. I think

you're crazy pretty. I would kill for blond hair and your legs. . . . I understand why you run. They're great!"

"Then why all this fuss over fixing me?"

"I just think you look like you don't care how you look, and you should." Stella added, "Maybe show it off a little."

The Three *T*s arrived right on time. "Show what off?" TJ asked.

"Oh, nothing," I said. "Just girl talk."

Tucker stood in the background behind TJ and Timmy. "I'm getting a funnel cake. Anyone want one?"

Timmy said to him, "Tuck, we have a workout in the morning."

Tucker said, "Duh. That's why I'm carb loading tonight."

"You carb loaded at lunch with pizza," TJ reminded him.

"Look, you prep for workouts your way, and I'll do it my way." To us he asked, "Funnel cake?"

"Well, I live for funnel cake," I said. I started digging a five-dollar bill out of my pocket.

Timmy whipped out a ten and gave it to Tucker. "I've got hers covered."

I don't think anyone else noticed, but I did—Timmy just bought me a funnel cake. A guy had never bought me anything before. Dario joined us, a little late to the party. "You got *me* covered, bro?" He laughed at himself like he'd made a joke, patted Tucker on the back, and said, "Just kidding. I'll go with you. I'm starving." As they walked away, Dario asked Tucker, "You have any idea how many refrigerator magnets I sold today? Have you ever met someone who says, 'Hey, while you're on vacation, can you pick up a magnet for me?'" Without letting Tucker answer, he said, "Me neither. And don't even get me started on snow globes. The thing about snow globes is this . . ."

I loved having these discussions with Dario, but I wasn't sure how Nifty Gifty topics were gonna go over with Tucker, who preferred talking about muscles and meat. I caught Stella making a slight eye roll.

TJ said, "Tuck's in for an earful, I think."

Timmy said, "Tuck hates heights, so I think we're safe to get in line without him. Should we wait for Dario?"

"He'll be sitting this out too," Stella said.

Timmy asked me, "You ready for this, Josie?"

"Ready, Freddie! It's better if I have funnel cake *after* the jump, so I don't—" I made a barfing imitation.

Timmy laughed and mimicked with the same. "You're funny."

People didn't usually describe me as funny.

"I like those sandals," he added. "And with three sisters, I see a lot of sandals."

I glanced at Stella, who smiled proudly at making my shoe selection for me. "Thanks." The compliment felt nice.

The line for the bungee snaked up a steep staircase. I

looked down at the fat mat below. "Can you imagine if someone missed that?" I asked.

Timmy said, "I don't want to."

"Me neither," a voice behind us said. It was Alayna Appleton, the Amazing Apple. "I mean, 'Hello, splat,'" she said.

I swear, just a quick wink before, she hadn't been in line behind us. How the heck did she do that?

"How do you do that?" TJ asked, echoing what everyone was thinking.

"Ancient magician secret," Apple said. We waited for her to continue. "It's SECRET, well, hello, that's why."

Luckily, we were at the top of the stairs and could easily switch the subject to who would jump first. Stella volunteered.

The bungee worker strapped a helmet on her and wrapped the harness around her waist.

"Here I go!" she exclaimed with nervous excitement. "See you at the bottom."

Right before Stella stepped off the ledge, TJ leaned into her and gave her a kiss on the cheek.

Before she could even react, she was flying over the edge in a perfect bungee.

Thirty-Seven

Police Station
June 26 (Continued)

"Amazing—um, I mean, Alayna Appleton—made a kissy sound that was totally immature." I pause, then add, "I couldn't believe it."

Detective Santoro leans on his elbows, his fists holding up his head. "The kissy sound or that Stella jumped?"

"We all jumped. That's what we were doing up there. Haven't you been paying attention? It was ripper cool, by the way. Such a shame Dario was too afraid. Have you tried it?"

"I have not," he says. "The kiss? Is that what bothered you?"

"No. I mean, it did, but not for the reason you're thinking."

"What am I thinking?" he asks me.

"You think I'm jealous that Stella is kissing someone and I'm

not." I don't tell him that I never have. That's not important to his investigation, and I really don't think he needs to know.

His expression is unchanged, totally flat. How does someone have only one expression? "You aren't jealous?"

"Maybe a little, not because she's with TJ, but because she isn't with me." I figure that needs explanation. "I mean, the summer is for me and Stella. That's the only time we see each other all year, and she's spending it with TJ, and she's pushing me to spend it with Timmy."

"I see," he says, again that expression. I think he still thinks I'm jealous that Stella kissed someone and I didn't.

I think about changing the subject by asking him about Laney and what he knows about that man from her phone. I'm not worried like Stella, but I'd feel better if I could just confirm it's her brother.

Instead I say, "That's when it happened again."

"Stella and TJ kissed again?"

"No. The pier."

Detective Santoro looks at me flatly, waiting to hear more.

"It moved. Again."

His brow lifts ever so slightly. Call in the Aussie Federal Police, Detective Frown Face showed an expression and raised a brow!

"After we jumped we landed one at a time on the fat mat . . . and I mean fat. Have you seen that thing? It's huge." I continue, "I was the last to go. I rolled myself off the mat and joined the others—Stella, TJ, and Timmy—who were waiting for me. It was such a rush; I mean, that jump is amazing. You have to try it."

He makes no indication that he plans to try the bungee.

"Dario and Tucker emerged from the crowd with funnel cake. Dario was asking Tucker, 'But why does anyone need another magnet? And have you ever wondered what's up with marshmallows? I'm not sure I care, because I'm gonna eat them anyway, but I'm curious: What's a marshmallow made of?' Stella's face turned a little red, like Dario was embarrassing her, and she tried to interrupt their convo by saying, 'Tucker might be interested in some of your Flying Fish research.' That's when Tucker handed me a paper plate covered with heavenly fried dough and powdered sugar. And Dario told us about the guys in the group—Evan, Austin, and Lucien. They're way involved with environmental protection efforts, volunteering to make marine habitats and stuff." I slip in, "Did I mention that Stella and TJ were holding hands?"

Detective Santoro doesn't comment on that. I think he might say it's kind of soon for that, since they, like, just started hanging out a few days ago. Instead he says, "The pier . . . it moved . . ."

"Oh, right." I explain. "So we listened to Dario tell us about the Flying Fish's environmental projects, and we shared funnel cake. That's when it happened again, just like last time."

"What did it feel like?"

"A sway. That's the best way to describe it. There was a mega wave, and it felt like the pier swayed a bit. TJ said, 'Whoa . . . feel that?' Timmy and Tucker were fighting over the last bite of funnel cake and asked, 'What?' Stella, Dario, and I shared a look, and

Dario whispered, 'Compromised.' Stella and I knew exactly what he meant, but the boys ignored him, because by this time Dario'd talked so much about things that they didn't really care about, except for the Flying Fish, that the guys had tuned him out." I add, *"Then the Three Ts had to leave."*

"Where were they going?"

"They didn't say." The boys don't know that we know where they've been. Detective Santoro writes something down, maybe that I don't know where the boys went; then he says, *"If the boys didn't think the sway was a big deal, maybe it wasn't. Maybe the movement was normal and really does happen all the time, except that since you had this idea in your minds about the pier's structural integrity, you made it into something that it wasn't?"*

I stare at him, because he is missing everything. "You aren't paying attention, Detective Santoro, and you're missing important clues."

He puts his pen down, rubs his hands over his face that's stubbled with a whisker shadow, and then leans back in his chair. "Please enlighten me, Josie."

"The jellies. The medusas. They were dying. *At Whalehead. And nowhere else!"*

Thirty-Eight

Josie

Mr. Rodney's Bungalow

June 24

"Murielle duPluie here with all the shore news on WLEO radio, and I'm happy to report that Meredith Maxwell has arrived in Whalehead. I repeat, Meredith Maxwell has arrived. Now, before you hunt her down for a selfie or autograph, you should know that her security is extensive because the rocker has an überfan that might be a little too über. At this time the overzealous fan's identity is unknown, but Maxwell's people are on a quest to find out.

"You'll have to admire the teen star from afar. Unless, like me, you've been invited to interview her during her promo event at the Smoothie Factory. Be sure to tune in to get the whole inside scoop on the music starlet."

Today we waited for the sun to burn off the morning dew and the walkers/joggers/Rollerbladers to finish their workouts before we went to see Mr. Rodney.

We heard Murielle duPluie's morning report from the loudspeaker that perched over the boards.

"Did you hear that?" Stella asked. "Meredith has extra security because of an überfan." She led the way down a path to the bungalow.

I said, "Hard to believe that she only has one. You know, being as famous as she is, right?" Then I knocked on Mr. Rodney's door, lightly, but apparently hard enough to push the door open.

"Mr. Rodney, are you here? It's Josie. I'm with Stella. Can we talk to you for a minute?" I moved my face toward the open crack.

And I couldn't believe what I saw.

Thirty-Nine

Police Station
June 26 (Continued)

"I pushed the door open, and I led the way into the bungalow. I told Stella, 'Don't be a wimp—just come on,' in order to make her come with me."

"Really?"

"Yeah. Stella had nothing to do with it. She's on the straight and narrow this summer. Not getting in any trouble. She doesn't know that I know this, but she had a rough year at school. But who can blame her? Her mom, Montana, got remarried, to Gregory. Did you know he goes by Gregory, not Greg?"

"I do."

"Anyway, that's a lot of change. Change stinks, you know? And then she had this other thing that happened with this guy

she's friends with. He's just a friend, not a boyfriend, and that's sort of the issue. Not really an issue, but a bummer, for sure."

Detective Santoro clears his throat. He's not into the details, which is weird for a detective, because you'd think he'd want to look closely at all the details. But not this guy. "Anyway, if she gets in trouble one more time, her mother is threatening to send her to a different school. Our dad told me. And that's why Stella is really careful, because she doesn't want to change schools. So, you see, she'd never do something like this unless I made her, which I did."

"Got it," he says. "Then what?"

I say, "One whole wall was wallpapered with photos and newspaper clippings."

"What kind of photos?"

"Medusas, the ocean, the pier, the water under the pier, a drainpipe under the pier, Meredith Maxwell."

"He had photos of Meredith Maxwell hanging on the wall?" He writes that down before I confirm.

"He's a fan too. Just like everyone else in Whalehead." I add, "On shelves he had a couple of framed photos of himself with a girl, a little girl. He looked all shaved and cleaned up in them. I think maybe it's his daughter."

"Why?"

"It was just the impression I got." I ask, "Do you have kids?" Dad never mentioned it. He's asking me lots of questions and getting to know me. Shouldn't I know him a little bit?

"Let's just stay focused, Josie." He calls me Josie, not Miss Higley this time, so maybe he's getting more comfortable with me, and he'll open up later, like when I tell him about the Minotaur Coaster. That's emotional, and emotional convos probably lead to more sharing.

I get back to what happened in the bungalow. "When I saw a drawing, I knew that Mr. Rodney had been following the same trail of bread crumbs we were."

"He draws?"

"Not well. But since I'd seen what he was drawing, I knew what it was. When we were snorkeling, I saw a drainpipe that empties local runoff into the ocean. It's under the pier. I guess he drew it because he didn't have an underwater camera." I add, "We have one at my school. It's owned by the marine conservation society. I'm running for prez this fall. Stella offered to make posters for me."

He writes that down. I'm not sure why he would need to remember that, but I'm touched that he cares.

"Lemme tell you about the other stuff we saw. Right there on a plastic table in the kitchen was a pile of paper folders among bunches of unopened mail. A real mess. Mr. Rodney is not a good housekeeper, not that I'm being judgy, just saying." I ask, "Are you? Do you like things neat?"

He leans his head right and left, making it crack.

"Anyway, I noticed on his mail that 'Rodney' is his first name, not last. All this time we've been calling him Mr. Rodney, like it's

his last name. And, get this, his mail is addressed to a doctor. He's a doctor of something. Who knew? But that's not important. What's important is those folders. You might wanna write this down."

He readies his pen.

"The first one got my attention because it said 'Medusas.' You know how worried I am about them. Then there was another one called 'Quotene.' That was a chemical analysis."

"How did you know that?"

"Because when I opened the folder, the paper said 'chemical analysis.'"

He doesn't look up from his notepad, but he pauses.

I spell: "Q-U-O-T-E-N-E."

Then he asks, "Anything else?"

"It had reports about Murphy's Pier. I didn't look at them closely until later. That's when I figured out they were measurements of the pylons."

He stops writing. "What do you mean, 'later'? Did you hang out there for a while?"

"No."

He waits, and when I don't answer right away, he puts his pen down. "Did you steal them?"

He leans back in his chair, and he does this thing where he lets the room be quiet. I can't stand it. There's only two of us here; one of us has to fill the awkward silence. It's not gonna be him. He's a stubborn man. So I say, "Steal? No. I took my phone out and snapped pics. We didn't take anything."

Forty

Josie

The Smoothie Factory

June 24 (Continued)

We made our way through the line at the Smoothie Factory for Stella to buy the elixir that symbolized everything wrong with this summer—the changes. I mean, what's wrong with keeping things the same? Especially when they're things we love, like Water Ice World? During the wait I devoured the information from the folders.

Stella said, "I feel the need to point out what an 'invasion of privacy' you said it was when I looked at Laney's camera roll." Stella imitated an Aussie accent with "invasion of privacy," and she was actually quite good. When we were kids, she used to pretend she was Australian. She doesn't know that I know. She continued, "But then you go ahead and copy all this stuff."

"It's not like these files were personal. Mr. Rodney—sorry, *Dr.* Rodney—and wants to figure out what's going on with the pier. Just like us. We have clues and so does he; it only makes sense that we put them together."

Stella said, "It makes sense that you'd ask him about it, not copy his stuff. Isn't that plagiarism?"

"Not exactly," I said. "I would love to ask him about it, but he's probably at some surf tourney. Who knows when he'll be back or how many jellies could die while we wait? I don't think you're understanding the urgency here."

"I do now that you've explained it," Stella said. "But maybe he doesn't know the urgency. We have his clues, but he doesn't have ours."

"I think he'll be proud of us for following his leads," I said.

Then, by some miracle, someone vacated a table, and I snatched it. Once Stella had paid for her evil concoction, she fell into the seat across from me. She sipped from the lime-green cup. "This is so insanely good. It's melon and blood orange, and there is this other flavor that I can't identify, but I love it. It's the same taste as last time. I think it's their secret sauce."

"I'm sure," I said, not looking up from the file.

With a straw wedged in the corner of her mouth, Stella asked, "So what've we got in there?"

"There's this chemical, quotene. It's organic. Looks like

Dr. Rodney—*Doctor?* It's gonna take a little while to get used to that—sent it to a lab and had it analyzed under a bunch of different conditions." Then I said, "The report shows that in some of the tests it's toxic."

Without removing the straw from the corner in which it was implanted, she said, "Toxic is never good. Right?"

"I think it's safe to assume it's generally bad." I added, "Especially since it was in the ocean where we swim and snorkel, and where fish live. Dr. Rodney got the sample from under the pier." I pointed to a map that I'd copied from the folder, where he'd marked an *X* on the spot where he'd taken the samples.

Stella unclenched her lips from the straw and said, "Toxins. That's also what he was looking for at the arcade."

"Yup."

Instead of speculating more about organic chemicals, she said, "Seriously, Jo, this is so good, so so good. You have to try it." Before I could protest, she said, "I know what you're gonna say, but ignore all of that for just a hot sec and taste this. No one at Water Ice World will ever know."

Just to shut her up, so that I could get to the other folders, I took a sip. "There. Happy?"

"Good, isn't it?"

I let the smoothie roll over my tongue.

A spark of lightning or something flashed in my brain, not because of the übernutrition, but because the taste ignited a memory—one that was deep down in the recesses of my childhood. I took the cup from Stella and tasted the smoothie again.

"I told you," she said, so satisfied that she was right about the smoothies. "Now you understand why everyone is hooked on these."

I didn't respond, because I was hyper-focused on the clear tubes of PVC pipe through which ribbons of purple liquid blended with the colorful fruits, while my mind was somewhere else entirely.

I'm a little girl, maybe six or seven, in Australia with my mom. We're traipsing along a dune near the beach and stop at a bush. My mom picks a berry for me. It tastes as if a peach and a grape had a purple baby.

I snapped my focus back onto Stella. "It's wattle berry," I said.

"What is?" Stella snatched the lime-green cup back from me like she was afraid that I'd finish it.

"Everything," I said. "It's all about wattle berries."

"What?" Stella was still confused.

"This drink is melon, blood orange, and *wattle berry*," I clarified. "It's from Australia."

Stella planted the straw back into its parking spot in the corner of her mouth, more interested in finishing the smoothie before I asked for more. "Never heard of it."

"There's a reason for that. The Australian Ecological

Society petitioned the gov to make the farming of wattle berries illegal when it was discovered that the berries are poisonous to certain species with sensitive digestive systems."

Stella picked up a napkin and spit out the smoothie that was in her mouth. "Poisonous? I've had like three—"

"Don't worry. It only hurts certain species with super-super-sensitive digestive systems. Not humans. There's a frog in southern Australia and—"

"Medusa jellyfish?" Stella asked.

"Right. There was some debate, because wattle berries are so nutritious—like, off the charts. Once scientists proved that the same health benefits could be found in other natural alternatives, they granted the petition and made harvesting the berries illegal. Aussies take environmentalism very seriously, and they follow that law. Wattle berries are quite rare and can only be found growing spontaneously in the wild here and there."

"How would Mrs. Gardiner, owner of the Smoothie Factory, like a bajillion miles away, in Whalehead, New Jersey, get an illegal, sometimes toxic berry from Australia? I mean, come on, Josie, your imagination is making this bizarre connection because you hate this place so much."

"That would mean that she has some suppliers from Australia—" I thought about the Australian guy that Lydia had told us about.

Stella said, "And the supplier has some way to transport the berries around the world."

My mind went to the *Koala*.

Stella said, "And he'd need local help."

Now I thought about the Three *T*s and the Water Sport Adventure van.

Stella said, "Really, Jo, it's ridiculous.

"Maybe not," I said. "If the processing of wattle berries creates an organic chemical called quotene, then Dr. Rodney hasn't concocted some crazy conspiracy this time. He knew something was affecting the medusas; he just didn't know what, or where it was coming from; that's why he was looking in the arcade," I said.

"Let's say the wattle berries are killing jellyfish. Who's dumping smoothies into the ocean?" Stella asked. "They're way too expensive, not to mention yummy, to throw them away."

"This place." I indicated the Smoothie Factory. "They're using wattles. The machine we saw in the basement is processing the berries. The berry waste goes into the drain we saw in the floor, and then it dumps into the ocean through the sewer pipe. Do you know where that pipe is?"

"I do," Stella said, to my surprise. She pointed to the *X* on Dr. Rodney's map on my phone. "I saw it when we were snorkeling."

"Yup. And what else is under the pier?" I asked.

"The pylons that have less wax." She rubbed her hands together and summarized: "Wattle berries are processed in the basement, creating a by-product called quotene, which drains into the water under Murphy's Pier. The medusa jellyfish consume it and die, because their bellies can't handle the toxin. And it also eats away at the wax on the pylons, damaging the stability of the pier."

I tilt my head at her. "You've been paying attention."

"See, I can be interested in boys *and* saving the world at the same time," Stella added.

The alarm on my phone buzzed.

"I'll do it," Stella said, and she texted Dad our location along with a selfie. She showed it to me.

I pointed to the girl who she'd captured in the background. "Who's that? She looks familiar."

"I never forget a face," Stella said. "That's Meredith Maxwell's number one fan. We signed the poster she made."

"Right. I remember. That's a cool job, running a fan club," I said. "What do we do next?"

Stella said, "I can think of two things."

Forty-One

Josie

Police Station

June 26 (Continued)

"The first thing I wanted to do was herd the medusas to safer water, like the Pied Piper of Jellies, but I was pretty sure there was no way to do that, and I was also pretty sure that wasn't what Stella was referring to."

"What did she want to do?" Detective Santoro asks.

"She wanted to cut off the wattle berry supply and get the pier shut down before the Flying Fish concert in three days, because, according to Dr. Rodney's calculations, the pier wouldn't support the weight of all those people now that the pylons had been compromised by the quotene."

"Getting Whalehead to close the pier is a big deal. How were you going to do that?"

"We needed help from someone with authority."

"So you went to talk to the mayor?"

"Not just yet, because a man entered the Smoothie Factory. Stella followed him with her eyes as he walked around the line of waiting smoothie wanters and behind the counter. 'Hold everything,' Stella said."

Forty-Two

Josie

The Smoothie Factory
June 24 (Continued)

"Stella, what are you looking at?"

"I know that guy." She shuffled for her phone and swiped the screen. She held it out for me. "See."

It was the man from Laney's phone.

"Who is he?" I asked.

"Dunno. Don't look now, but—" Stella snapped her fingers in front of my face. "Listen, do not look. Got it?" She pointed to her eyes. "Look here."

"Okay."

"Outside the window, a woman in a baseball hat and sunglasses is watching that dude."

I started turning my head toward the window, but Stella snapped her fingers.

"Hey." She pointed to her eyes. "Here."

I did what she said. "It's Laney, isn't it?"

Stella nodded.

Forty-Three

Police Station

June 26 (Continued)

"You're talking about Laney Marini? The one I arranged for your dad to meet?"

"Yeah. Sorry, but Stella never trusted her. And it looks like Stella was right, because Laney's definitely up to something. How well do you know her?"

He wiggles in his seat a little.

This is the first time Detective Santoro seems uncomfortable, so he's hiding something too.

"Wait. You do know her, don't you? You didn't set my dad up with some random stranger."

"We're colleagues. I know her." He searches his notebook for

some other questions to ask me. "Look, let's stay on track. What did you think she was doing?"

I say, "We have theories. . . ."

"What kind of theories?"

"She was a private detective, and that man's wife had hired her to follow him, to see if he was having an affair. Or the two of them were a team planning to rob the Smoothie Factory on the day it would make millions of dollars. So the guy was posing as a deliveryman to scope out the details of the shop."

"You think like a cop," he says, and I think he means it as a compliment.

"It was ridiculous at first, but the more we thought about it, the more it seemed like a great way to steal a lot of money in one day."

"Plausible."

"If you think it's plausible, it means that you don't even know enough about her to know that she's not planning some kind of major robbery, but you set her up with my dad anyway?" I cross my arms.

He doesn't answer.

"Can I ask you something?"

Again no answer, but I ask anyway, "Are you a good detective?"

He shrugs like he's being modest but he thinks he's good.

"I don't want to worry that you'll become a matchmaker."

Forty-Four
Josie

Boardwalk—Whalehead, New Jersey
June 24 (Continued)

We agreed to save the jellies and potential concertgoers before saving the Smoothie Factory from a robbery.

We figured that Officer Booth wouldn't listen to us, and that left Mayor Lopez as the person with authority to help us.

I called his office. They said that he was on the pier trying out the new bungee for a segment on WLEO, so to the pier we went.

I shielded my eyes from the sun. "There he is," I said, looking up to the jump platform. He was being dramatic, pretending to be scared, showing off. Murielle duPluie's microphone was extended on a long pole from about three-quarters of the way up the stairs, like that was as far up as she could handle.

A small crowd had gathered around the safety mat, waiting for the mayor to bounce on it. And they weren't disappointed when he plopped, laughing the whole time. He shimmied himself off the mat, and by the time he'd unhooked his gear, Murielle was next to him, ready to bring his commentary to her radio listeners.

duPluie: Tell us how you're feeling right now.
Lopez: I'm a little winded, actually. It was so exciting, it took my breath away.
duPluie: Were you scared?
Lopez: Nah. That was just an act. I'm the brave type.

He puffed out his chest.

Lopez: But if I didn't know that this huge mat was down here, that'd be a different story.
duPluie: Would you do it again?
Lopez: Absolutely. This ride is worth every penny and a great addition to the attractions Whalehead offers on Murphy's Pier. This is just another reason for vacationers to choose our beach.

From a little distance, a voice yelled to the mayor, "What about the dead jellyfish? Are you aware they're being poisoned? What are you going to do about it?" It was none other than our mate Dr. Rodney, apparently back from whatever surf competition or chemical analysis he'd been doing.

Officer Booth was on Dr. Rodney before he could spurt out another question. "That's enough now, Hot Rod. This is about the bungee ride, not allegedly poisoned jellyfish or one of your other half-baked ideas."

The mayor called over to Officer Booth, "It's okay. I want to answer that." He leaned in to Murielle's mic. "There appears to be a problem with the local species of medusa jellyfish. My office is aware of this. We're very concerned and have commissioned experts to assess the situation and give us a full report of their findings. Once we have that in hand, we'll review options and move ahead with the most aggressive approach."

Dr. Rodney started yelling something else, but Murielle regained control of her interview.

duPluie: Why wasn't the public informed about this?

Lopez: We didn't want to cause a panic. The water has been tested, and it's been confirmed that it's safe for swimming. My office will always put the safety of this community ahead of all else.

duPluie: How will the town pay for all of this?

Lopez: Thanks to our conservative budgeting practices, we have money in reserve for such disasters. A good local government always plans ahead.

He smiled and searched the small crowd as if looking for the TV camera or photographer for a photo op, but there was neither.

Lopez: Speaking of local government, I have to get back to work. Thank you, Ms. duPluie and everyone at WLEO.

duPluie: Oh no, thank *you,* Mr. Mayor. And also I want to compliment you about your office providing a hotel room for Meredith Maxwell's fan club president, Cassandra Winterhalter. That's very generous.

Lopez: It's important to the community that celebrities feel welcomed here in Whalehead. We want them to come back, right? So when Miss Winterhalter approached my office about finding accommodations when everything was sold out, we helped. I mean, without her, who will lead Maxwell's local fans?

duPluie: Too true, Mr. Mayor.

Forty-Five

Josie

Boardwalk

June 24 (Continued)

Once the mayor was off the air and the crowd had dissipated, many of them jumping in line for the bungee, Stella and I approached him.

He smiled when he saw us, like always. "Hi, girls. What are you up to today? Planning a bonfire for tonight?"

"There's a bonfire tonight?" Stella asked. "I hadn't heard about it." It was just like Stella to lose focus at the mention of a social opp. She was plagued with FOMO.

"Not sure. I thought you guys did that most nights."

I said, "That was nice of you to get a hotel room for Meredith Maxwell's number one fan."

He said, "When you're the mayor, sometimes you can pull strings."

"Very cool." Then I got us back on track. "We actually wanted to talk to you about something serious."

"Something serious?" He looked right at us. "What's up?"

"It's related to the jellies, actually," I said.

"Okay . . . what is it?"

"I—I mean, *we*—think that the jellies are being killed because their digestive systems can't handle a certain chemical under the pier. And the same chemical is damaging the pylons. And damaged pylons won't hold up the weight of all the people on the pier when they come to the Flying Fish concert."

Mayor Lopez pulled his sunglasses out of his front breast pocket and put them on. "I see," he said. "Digestive systems. Chemicals. Pylons." He seemed to think about this. "Any chance you girls have been talking to Rodney?"

Stella and I looked at each other. I suddenly thought about the files we'd relied on for these theories. What if those were bogus or made up?

"That's what I thought." He headed toward the boardwalk. "Look, girls, have you ever heard the expression 'consider the source'? I think that applies here. Rod has a history of sending our law enforcement on wild-goose chases, and that's a very inefficient way for me to manage our town."

"But—"

He kept walking. "I really do have experts coming in.

We'll see what they say. Now I have to get to work." Mayor Lopez sped up and started talking to a few other folks nearby. Clearly the conversation was over.

I looked at Stella. "That didn't go well."

"No," she said as she watched something in the distance. "Plan B?"

"What's plan B?"

She nodded toward Officer Booth, who was pouring sugar into his coffee.

"Ugh. I don't think so. He hates Dr. Rodney. What's he gonna do?"

"Booth's a cop. He might be more likely to listen to evidence."

I shrugged. "It's not like we have anything to lose. The worst that could happen is that he could laugh at us."

Stella said, "He probably will."

"Probably."

I walked slowly on our approach, letting Stella be slightly in front of me.

"Hey there, Officer Booth," Stella said. "It's a great day, isn't it? No such thing as a bad day at the beach, that's what I always say."

He didn't smile or make any move to indicate that he was anything other than annoyed that we were interrupting his coffee.

"What do you want?" he asked. "I'm kinda busy."

"We need help from an experienced investigator, like yourself."

"Is that so?" He blew steam off his coffee.

"You see, we've been gathering some information about the pier, and it seems like the integrity of the pylons—"

He chuckled. "Their *integrity*? Is that a word you found in your information?"

As we'd suspected, he was laughing at us.

"It is." Stella remained cool. For now. It's not like Stella to keep cool for long. "And it says that the pylons are wearing away and won't be able to support the weight of all the people who will be on the pier for the Flying Fish concert."

He spit his hot coffee onto the ground and laughed out loud this time. "Sure it does." When he saw that we weren't laughing along, he looked at his watch and said, "Look, I got a lot going on today, girls."

I didn't believe that. I figured what he had going on was coffee here on the pier, maybe a walk to Moe's for another coffee, then back to the pier to finish his day with coffee. "Just listen to us," Stella said. "Geez, this is real."

"It's *evidence*," I assured him.

"And where did you get this *evidence* from?"

Stella and I exchanged a look, because as soon as we told him it was Dr. Rodney's research, he'd disregard its value.

"Let me guess. You got it from a ramshackle shed. Probably it was papered with photos of flying saucers. Maybe a poster that says 'The Truth Is Out There.' Am I right?" He tipped the hot coffee into his mouth.

"No." I propped my hands on my hips. "As a matter of fact, you are wrong with a big, fat capital *W*."

Stella interrupted me. "Jo—"

I ignored her, but not the fact of our role reversals. I was losing my cool, and Stella was trying to stop me. It's probably not a bad thing that Stella and I rub off on each other, because I can be too timid, and she can be too aggressive.

I said, "He's a big Flying Fish fan, and he had posters of Meredith Maxwell in his *bungalow*—it's not a shed."

Officer Booth swallowed the hot coffee too fast, because he clenched his neck like it hurt his throat. "You say he has pictures of Maxwell?" He set his coffee on the ledge of a whack-a-mole midway game.

The worker said, "Dude, that's gonna spill."

Booth glanced over the top of his aviator sunglasses, and whatever look he gave intimidated the worker enough for him to surrender with both hands.

Booth pulled out his smartphone. While he tapped a message, he said, "I wouldn't pay much attention to what Rod says." Booth pointed to his head. "Fried. Too much sun and surf fried the guy's brain." He used his finger to stir his coffee, wincing at its heat, and licked it off quickly. "Why don't you girls go build a sand castle, or chew gum, or something like normal kids do at the beach?"

I fumed. "Jellies are DYING! And all these people"—I swung my arm around to highlight the tourists and workers on Murphy's Pier—"are in danger, and they don't even know it." My voice got louder. "And you don't care!"

Booth slowly returned his phone to his pocket, straightened his posture, and took off his sunglasses. He bent down to be at our eye level. "Look, Josie Higley, I highly recommend you chill out." Then he swung the darts over to Stella. "And you, Stella Higley, don't get started. Get off this pier before I bring you two to the station for disturbing the peace. And if you don't think I'll do it, I dare you to test me. It would be the highlight of my day." He stood back up, returned his sunglasses to his face, and asked, "Clear?"

Stella sucked in a breath like she was gonna shout at him, but I grabbed her forearm.

Dodging eye contact, I mumbled, "Clear," a beat before Stella did.

Booth picked up his coffee and casually walked off.

When he was far enough away that he couldn't hear, I said to Stella, "One thing is clear."

"Totally. Let's do it," Stella said.

Stella and I were on the same page for what felt like the first time this summer. In sync. And that felt good.

Forty-Six

Josie

Police Station
June 26 (Continued)

"Before you tell me more about Booth, can you tell me what you thought of Meredith Maxwell's number one fan?"

"Cassandra? At that time I thought it was nice that Mayor Lopez was able to use his connections to get her a hotel room." Later, I understood more about how a mayor pulling strings isn't always a good thing, but I don't want Detective Santoro to know about that.

"Did you know where Booth was going?" Detective Santoro asks me.

"No. But he was on a mission, so I assumed some kind of official police business."

"Did the pictures in Rodney's bungalow concern you? The pics of Maxwell."

"I didn't think twice about them. I just thought he liked the Flying Fish. Who doesn't, right?"

Detective Santoro turns back a page in his little flippy notebook. "What did you mean when you said one thing was clear?"

I pick at my cuticle without answering.

"What was clear, Josie?"

I think I should be careful with this answer. Detective Santoro might be my dad's fishing mate, but he's also a law enforcement guy. So, essentially he and Booth and the mayor are all on the same team.

"Josie? What was clear?"

"That Booth and the mayor didn't believe us."

"Meaning what?"

"They weren't going to help." I stare at his unsmiling face. (Has this guy ever smiled in his life?) I glance at the dirty linoleum floor. "So, you see, we had to."

"Had to what?"

I realize my fingers have turned white because I'm holding the table so hard. I stare deep into his chestnut-colored eyes. "Time was running out. We had to take matters into our own hands. Jellies were dying; people were in danger. We had no choice, Detective Santoro."

Forty-Seven

Josie

Boardwalk

June 24 (Continued)

We had a plan.

First we wanted to shut down the incoming wattle berry supply, and to do that we had to learn more about the process that was going on at night.

"How are we gonna do that?" I asked Stella.

"A stakeout."

That night Stella and I returned to the boardwalk to spy on the Three *T*s.

Somehow their nightly kayaking trip put them in the middle of this. They probably had no idea that they were in cahoots with the scheme that had so many terrible down-stream effects. If they did, they never would've been involved.

The boardwalk was different after dark. The music from the merry-go-round was louder; the smell of burgers was stronger; exercisers were replaced by ice cream eaters. Couples strolled hand in hand on the boards and barefoot on the beach. The birds had gone to bed. One thing was the same. It was always in the background: the laughs and giggles of people on vacation. The good cheer floated through the air, and that's what made the shore feel like the shore.

I confirmed that we hadn't forgotten anything. "Binoculars?" I asked Stella.

She pulled them out of the backpack. "Check. Three pairs."

"Flashlight?"

"Check."

"Cell phone?"

"Check."

"Notebook and pen?"

"Check and check."

Dario ran down the boardwalk, paper plate in his hand, catching the end of our list. "Funnel cake? Check. It would be inhumane to have a stakeout without it." He broke off a piece of fried dough and ate it. "I'm pretty sure this is a doughnut in disguise. What's the deal with jam filling anyway? It just ends up on your shirt. I don't think I've ever eaten a jam-filled doughnut and actually eaten the jam. It always lands on my shirt, but that doesn't stop me from getting them. It's like a challenge now. The cream filling isn't as bad; it doesn't move as fast on account of it being less slippery—"

I broke off a piece of funnel cake while Stella rolled her eyes. She said, "Can we stick to the task here—stakeout, not doughnut wars?"

Dario's eyes bulged. "I love that idea. It could be like *Game of Thrones* with a whole army of doughnuts fighting an army of partially chewed zombie doughnuts. They would say, 'Morning is coming,' because people mostly eat doughnuts in the morning, which, when you think about it, doesn't really make any sense, because it is, after all, a cake, so essentially a dessert food." He pushed the record button on his phone to capture an audio memo. "Feature news segment idea: Why do people eat doughnuts for breakfast? Uh, scratch that. Make it, why don't people eat doughnuts for dessert?"

Stella said, "Stakeout. Focus. It will be midnight, and we'll still be here talking about doughnuts. Don't forget Dad wants us home before eleven."

I told Dario, "Doughnuts will have to wait."

"Fine." Then he asked me, "How are we gonna do this?"

Stella clicked an app on her phone. "This app tells me the location of all of my connections. See, it's a dot with the person's name under it. Since TJ and I are connected, as long as he has his phone on him, I can see where he is." She watched a map of Whalehead open, and a dot blinked, indicating her position, and then other dots blinked, showing where her online friends were. There was one for me and one for Dario—right next to hers—and Angie's dot was moving up Ocean Drive. Then we saw TJ's. It was with Timmy's and Tucker's.

"Are they night swimming?" Dario asked.

"Nope," Stella said. "Kayaking."

"Let's get into position," I said. Then I looked at the dots on my phone's app. Stella and I had a lot of the same connections, except for one, because I had an extra dot. I hovered over it to see who it was. It was Laney, and she was nearby.

I looked down the boardwalk and saw her in her Phillies baseball cap. She leaned on the railing between the Smoothie Factory and Kevin's Fun House, the section that's right above our secret spot with the kayak groove. She looked through a telescope, giving the appearance she was stargazing.

Stella didn't trust her, and I was beginning to think Stella's instincts were right, because things were coming together for me about Laney. I remembered:

- the cap from Ocean Avenue the other night;
- the man from the Smoothie Factory who was on her phone;
- her pictures of the *Koala*.

I didn't know why, but she was also following the wattle berries. We walked down to the beach. We had to walk slow so Dario could keep up—he was challenged with balancing fried dough on a plate.

"Here looks good," Stella said. She dropped to her knees, lay on her belly, and took the binoculars out of the pack.

Dario and I lay on either side of her.

She handed a pair to me but hesitated to give a pair to Dario.

"What's the problem?" he asked.

She looked at his hands. "Sticky."

He set the paper plate on the sand in front of him, licked his hands, and wiped them on his butt. "Clean."

"Gross," Stella said, but gave him the third pair anyway.

I said, "You need to stop at one of your favorite soap spots later."

We glued the binoculars to our faces.

Dario said, "Moe's is in the lead, by the way. Theirs smells like cucumber ginger."

"Shh." Stella stared through the binoculars. "They're out there somewhere."

We were quiet for a quick wink while we all scanned the dark ocean.

Then, out of the blue, from my left, a new voice said, "I love a good stakeout."

We three dropped our binoculars and looked at the sudden appearance of Apple lying next to us.

"Hey," she said. She broke off a piece of fried dough from the plate in front of her and chewed it. She opened her mouth and showed us the chewed-up food. "Hello, zombie funnel cake," she said.

Dario laughed. "Exactly."

"This reminds me of when I was at summer camp in Zimbabwe."

Dario asked, "You went to camp in Zimbabwe?"

"Very exclusive. A place to learn the ancient art of Magoola-goo-goo. That's a form of magic dating back to the dawn of man. It's taught by a transcendental warrior king from the Neolithic era."

"How does this remind you of that?" I asked even though I doubted Apple had gone to these exotic places.

"They have night. It gets dark, and there's sand. And birds. Not gulls, of course, winged woolly mammoths that sound like gulls. We'd watch their synchronized flight with binoculars."

"Shh," Stella said again. "We have serious work to do." It always surprised me that Stella didn't call Apple out about these far-fetched trips.

I put the binoculars back to my face and studied the ocean.

"Fine," Apple said. She didn't talk anymore, but she chewed with her mouth open. I swear I could smell the tuna she'd had earlier.

"There," Stella said. She pointed out farther than I'd been looking. "See the lights? It's a boat. The kayaks are to the right of it. See it?"

"Got it," I said. People on the kayaks were taking bags from someone off the back of the boat.

"I can't see the person on the boat. But I think it's a man," Dario said.

"For sure," I said.

A cloud covering the moon floated aside, providing some light, but by then the man had turned his back.

"See the name of the boat?" Stella asked.

"Yup."

"Sound familiar?" she asked.

"Nope," Dario said.

"Yup," I said again.

We got Dario up to speed about what we knew about the *Koala*.

Forty-Eight

Josie

Boardwalk

June 25

> "Murielle duPluie here with breaking news from WLEO. Our own Whalehead police have taken Dr. Rodney Klinger in for questioning under suspicion of his stalking Meredith Maxwell. The teen rock star is moving ahead with her promo event and interview session at the Smoothie Factory, while the rest of the band–Evan, Austin, and Lucien–are on the pier with a crew to build the set for their concert."

We stood on the boardwalk by the post where a loudspeaker played WLEO, and we listened to Murielle duPluie's report.

"That's our fault," I said.

"Yup," Stella agreed. "We should've been way more careful what we told Booth."

"What do you think will happen to Dr. Rodney?"

"He's just being questioned. Dr. Rodney is a little weird, but I don't think he's a stalker. Do you?" Stella asked.

"No. But how do you explain those photos? Why all the interest in Meredith?"

"There has to be another reason. Maybe he really is a huge fan," Stella suggested, but I didn't even think she believed it.

A crowd formed, and people moved toward the Smoothie Factory.

"Where are they all going?" I asked.

"To see Meredith Maxwell."

As sure as the smell of fries drifted through the air, she finally arrived. She was prettier in person, albeit a little shorter than I'd imagined. She wore distressed, white cropped jeans and a sleeveless top that hung short in the front, just above her waist, and longer in the back. Her brownish-blond-ombré hair was adorned with beachy braids and twists. Meredith was flanked by two burly men in black pants and white T-shirts that were tight on their chests, and biceps that Tucker could only dream of having one day.

"I can't believe she's doing a promo shoot for that place.

She has no idea what type of a business she's supporting," I said. "If she knew, there's no way she'd do it."

We watched for a beat, and I got an idea. "That's it! Stell, we'll tell her what they're doing and tell her how dangerous the concert is. It's so simple. Once she knows, she'll help us."

Meredith looked at the array of fans gathered and waved. "Hello, Whalehead," she cried. "I'm doing a quick video shoot in my favorite spot for a cold, healthy drink, and then I plan on having a little fun, if you know what I mean." She pointed to Kevin's Fun House. "After that I'll be back at the Factory to mix some of my own concoctions and talk with your local media, then call it a day. I want to thank everyone for welcoming me, and also I want to thank"—she leaned her ear toward a woman who offered a whisper—"Cassandra Winterhalter?"

"Over here!" a voice screamed out from the crowd, but it was tough to tell exactly who it came from.

Meredith said, "Cassandra is the head of my local fan club and led the effort for my welcome poster that many of you were kind enough to sign. I'll cherish it always." With another wave, she ducked inside the Smoothie Factory while her men guarded the door.

"Oh, she's so super nice," I said. "I'm sure that if we told her what was going on, she could fix everything. She'd totally cancel the concert, and Mayor Lopez would listen to *her* and close the pier."

"Yup. We just have to explain it to her, and everything will be fine. But how?" Stella asked.

I said, "If only we could get her alone for a few minutes."

Stella said, "She'll be in the Smoothie Factory shooting her video, then the fun house."

Forty-Nine

Josie

Police Station

June 26 (Continued)

"And that's when I got the idea. I told Stella how we could get Meredith's attention."

"What did you tell Stella?"

"My plan: to go to Kevin's Fun House ahead of Meredith, and when she got to the trapdoor, we'd bring her under the boardwalk and tell her everything. Once she knew, she'd help us expose the Smoothie Factory, the danger on the pier, cancel or postpone the concert, and everything would be fixed. I mean, we were on the verge of disaster without a lot of options."

"It was your idea, Josie?"

"Yeah. Stella didn't want to do it. She said it was a bad idea, but I told her not to be a wimp."

Detective Santoro looks carefully at the pages of his little flippy notebook. "Miss Higley, are you saying that you made a plan to kidnap Meredith Maxwell?"

"Kidnap? No. That was Meredith Maxwell's word." I stop to think. "It sounds really bad when you say it that way."

"How would you say it?"

"We just wanted to talk to her. Privately. We would never kidnap anyone."

He does that thing where he lets the room be quiet. I hate that thing.

I'm basically forced to say more. "To ask for her help."

He shifts in his seat. "This was your plan?"

"All mine. Totally. One hundred percent. I'm like a mastermind."

Part Three

Stella

Fifty

Stella

Police Station

June 26 (Continued)

"Things were moving fast now. The concert was, like, forty-eight hours away. We needed to act," I say. "I told Josie how we could get Meredith alone."

"Your idea?" Santoro confirms.

"Yup." I add, "Josie didn't like it at all. She didn't want to do it."

Santoro flips open his notebook. This is the juicy part he's been waiting for. "What did you want to do?"

"Approach Meredith Maxwell for help."

"How?"

"By getting her attention. Talking to her alone."

"How were you going to do that?"

"She was going to Kevin's Fun House after the Smoothie

Factory." I add, "I planned to get her under the boardwalk, where we could talk in private."

"So, let me get this straight, Stella. You planned to kidnap Meredith Maxwell?"

"I don't know why everyone is using that word. Meredith was being way dramatic on the pier," I explain. "More like borrow."

"And Josie went along with this?"

"Heck no. You see, Josie plans to run for president of her school's marine conservation society in the fall. And she wouldn't do anything wrong. Nothing to jeopardize that." I add, "This was all me."

Fifty-One

Stella

Under the Boardwalk

June 25 (Continued)

We were hiding among the foam pillars when we heard Meredith Maxwell coming. As I'd thought, her big beefy bodyguards couldn't fit. She said to them, "I'll meet you at the exit." One of them grunted in agreement.

Meredith wiggled through the pillars, and when she scaled the rope bridge, we were right behind her. I did a quick slide of the barrel, and a hot sec later Meredith's butt landed on the sand in our secret place under the boardwalk. Josie and I were right behind her.

"Hey," I said to her.

"Sorry about that," Josie said, pointing to the hard sand.

Meredith's face was bright red. And it wasn't from the sun. "What the heck!? Who are you people?"

"I can't believe you're here." Josie looked as if Santa had just brought her the pink bike with sparkly tassels hanging off the handlebars that she'd been dying for.

Meredith stood and assumed a defensive martial arts pose with her legs apart and arms up. "Bring it. I'm trained. I can totally take you two." She looked me up and down. "Especially you."

"I'm stronger than I look." I straightened up. "And I'm from New York, so—"

"Ohhh, New York. That makes, like"—she paused and spit out—"no difference at all! What do you want? A picture? An autograph? Me to go to your birthday party?"

Josie said, "I imagined you to be much friendlier than this." Then she added, "We just wanna talk to you. We have something super important that you're gonna want to hear."

Josie seemed to relax Meredith a little. Her accent had that effect on people.

"You're obviously not from New York," Meredith said. "Australia?"

Josie nodded.

"Cool. I love it there." Meredith dropped her arms, as if the fact that Josie was an Aussie indicated that she was no longer in danger, which it did. Well, she never was.

There were the sounds of feet stomping overhead. "Hear

that?" Meredith asked. "There are people looking for me. I could yell right now."

"Are you kidding me?" I asked. "It sounds like that all the time: joggers, skateboarders who aren't supposed to be skateboarding, crying kids, loud music, the merry-go-round. Go ahead and yell—no one will notice." I took out my phone and checked the time. "We have another good twelve minutes before people wonder why you haven't come out of the fun house." I didn't totally believe this, but it sounded like it could be true, although it was equally possible that some of those footsteps were people running around frantically looking for Meredith. Also, while I had my phone out, I noticed it was close to the time we should check in with Dad. I dropped him a text and showed Josie, so she would know I did it.

Josie nodded about the text, then said, "She's right. There's a lot to see and do in the fun house, so we have time."

"Look," I said. "We didn't mean to scare you; we just really needed to get you alone, because this is way important. Life or death."

"Well, there are probably better ways to do that other than kidnapping," she said. "Because now you're gonna be in, like, insanely big trouble."

"Kidnapping?" Josie asked, incredulous. "That isn't what this is."

I thought about the last few minutes. "Maybe that's what it feels like, but it's not like that at all. You aren't in any danger."

"Just being held against my will," Meredith said sarcastically.

"You know, you're really being extra right now," I said.

Josie added, "And no one is holding anyone. You can leave anytime you want."

"Fine. Then I want to leave right now."

"Sure," I said, stepping into her path. "As soon as you listen to this."

"See, *that's* against my will."

Josie said, "If you'll just listen, this will only take a quick wink."

Meredith crossed her arms in front of her chest and tapped her foot like she didn't have time for this. We hadn't considered that Meredith would be such a jerk. "Well, go on. I'm a celebrity with a very busy schedule."

"Here's the deal—" I started.

"No," she interrupted me. "*You* tell me," she said to Josie. "I don't like *you*," she said to me. And the feeling was mutual.

Josie looked at me. "It's okay. I got this." She went through the situation: The Smoothie Factory was making their amazing shakes using wattle berries from Australia, where farming the berries was banned because they're harmful to the ecosystem. Some guy was bringing berries to Whalehead on a boat called the *Koala*. When the Smoothie Factory processed the berries in its basement, it created an organic by-product that drained into the ocean.

"Two things happen when this chemical hits the water. It eats away at the pylons, which is damaging the stability of the pier, making it totally dangerous for people to be on it."

"And the second thing?" Meredith asked impatiently.

"The lovely medusa jellies ingest it, and their delicate digestive systems can't handle it, and they die." Josie added, "The medusas here in Whalehead are dying."

Meredith didn't say anything right away. I think she was contemplating how she should react:

Mean: *Oh, cry me a river.*

Sympathetic: *That's the saddest thing I've ever heard.*

What Meredith said was, "This is all very unbelievable, you know?"

"We have proof," Josie said.

Meredith noodled over this. "I can see why you're so worried, but what do you want me to do about it? I mean, what does any of this have to do with me?"

"No one will listen to us," I said.

Josie added, "But they'll listen to you."

"Fine. I'll tell the authorities, and you'll just let me go?"

"We aren't keeping you here; you can walk away anytime you want. Right there." I pointed to the sand path between the two buildings, which lead to Thirty-Fourth Street. She went to walk in that direction, and I stepped in front of her again. "You'll cancel the concert?"

"No one said anything about canceling the concert. I

can't cancel a concert! Do you know all the hype that this concert is getting?"

Josie said, "But the pier could collapse, and all those people, including you, will fall into the ocean! Think about your bandmates—Evan, Austin, and Lucien."

"Collapse?" Meredith asked Josie.

Josie nodded. "Look, you can leave. Stella, move out of her way. But we really hope you'll help us."

Josie did a great job pushing all the hot buttons—dead fish, dead fans, dead bandmates. I expected the next thing Meredith was going to do was agree to help.

The plan had worked perfectly.

But then, like all perfect things, something changed.

Fifty-Two

Stella

Under the Boardwalk

June 25 (Continued)

Someone else jumped down!

All the years that we'd been slipping through the trap-door from the fun house, this had never happened to us.

She knocked me over and landed on top of me.

"Who are you?" Josie asked.

"Seriously? You don't know who I am?" She looked at Meredith. "You do, right?"

Meredith didn't offer a name or hint of recognition.

The girl put her hand on her chest. "I'm Cassandra." She climbed off me.

I never forget a face. "Cassandra Winterhalter!" I exclaimed.

Cassandra tilted her head and said to Meredith, "I'm you're number one fan." After just a beat, she added, "I organized that welcome sign. Everyone signed it." She looked at me and Josie. "You two did. I remember."

"We did," Josie confirmed. "The first day."

"Well, gee, thanks," Meredith said. "That's . . . um . . . it's a great sign." It's a good thing Meredith was a good singer, because she was a terrible actress. I didn't believe for a hot sec that she thought that was a great sign or that she appreciated it.

Cassandra said, "And, as is my duty as your number one fan, I keep a close eye on you, even when you don't know it. And I noticed that you were in trouble, and I've come to rescue you."

"She totally is *not* in any trouble," I clarified as I wiped sand off my butt.

Josie assured Cassandra, "This is just a friendly convo."

"Oh really? Didn't look that way to me," Cassandra said.

"Look, I'm sorry to break up this little par-tay, but me and Meredith have someplace to be."

"We do?" Meredith asked.

"Yeah. I sent you a letter—don't you remember?"

Meredith said, "Um, yeah, sure I do." Again, terrible acting.

"Then let's go. I made a promise, and I'm gonna keep it," Cassandra said.

"What promise is that?" I asked. I figured we'd have to rescue Meredith from her number one fan, who seemed to be kidnapping her.

"That she and I would ride the Minotaur together," she said. "Let's do it."

"I don't know if now is the right time for us to do that," Meredith said. "I'm on a schedule for this promotional tour gig, and I have a hair appointment."

Cassandra ignored the hair appointment, took Meredith by the elbow, and said, "Just think of the photo op for your social media."

Meredith tilted her head as if Cassandra had made an interesting point. Then she winced from the tight squeeze. "Not so hard, though. I bruise."

"Sorry," Cassandra said. "But let's get going."

"Maybe we'll go with you," I suggested, because even though Meredith Maxwell was a jerk to us, and she swore that she had the ninja skills to get away if she wanted to, I felt responsible for this situation, and I wanted to try to help her, or at least keep her company.

Josie, understanding what I was trying to do, said, "Now, *that* sounds like wicked fun. Let's all go."

"No!" Cassandra snapped. "I am her number one fan. Not you." She narrowed her glare at us. "Don't you two mess this up for me. The photo caption will read, 'Meredith

Maxwell and her number one fan ride the world-famous Minotaur together.'"

As she led Meredith to Thirty-Fourth Street, I heard Cassandra whisper, "Where are we getting our hair done?"

Fifty-Three

Stella

Police Station

June 26 (Continued)

I sit forward in my seat and say to Santoro, "So, things get a little cray."

He straightens up, flips a page, and starts writing faster. "What happened?"

"Cassandra led Meredith down the sand alleyway to Thirty-Fourth Street. Before they were out of sight, she turned to me and Josie and said, 'Don't cross me, Stella and Josie Higley.'"

Santoro keeps writing this all down.

"She knew our names!"

"So you waited there?"

"No way!" I puff my chest out a bit. "You know what a New Yorker does when someone pushes them? We push back!"

Just one corner of his mouth lifts the tiniest bit.

"Now, Josie was another story; she isn't naturally the pushing type."

"So what did you do?" Santoro asks.

Fifty-Four

Stella

Boardwalk

June 25 (Continued)

We ran up the ramp from Thirty-Fourth Street to the boardwalk, where Murielle duPluie's coverage of the news was blaring through the loudspeaker situated high up on a pole, surrounded by vacationers listening to her report.

> "Murielle duPluie here with all the shore news from WLEO. I have breaking news.
>
> "This just in: Meredith Maxwell's security detail has lost contact with her, and they've gone into Kevin's Fun House to find her. Flying Fish bandmate Austin Barry is asking everyone to look for the starlet."

We ran to the Minotaur and didn't hear the rest of the report.

"There she is!" someone in the crowd cried, and a sea of Good Samaritans ran toward the pier in an effort to rescue her, but we were ahead of them, nearly at the coaster, where Cassandra was leading Meredith onto a cart.

We could just make out their voices over the *bam! bam! bam!* of helicopter blades.

Meredith yelled, "We can take the picture down here."

"Up there is better." Cassandra pointed to the peak of the coaster. "A perfect spot for two besties to get a one-of-a-kind shot."

The cart edged higher to the peak before it would speed down a steep hill. But then, just as the cart got to the top, it stopped.

"What happened?" I asked.

Josie shaded her eyes from the sun. "It stopped, or I think it's stuck, maybe?"

The Three *T*s ran down the pier in their red lifeguard shirts. Dario was behind them. The *T*s had been running in sand all summer, so Dario had no chance of keeping up with them.

"What's going on?" Timmy asked Josie.

She gave him the summary, obviously leaving out the part where Meredith thought that we were kidnapping her. No one really needed to know that part. "And," Josie said to Timmy, "when this is over, we need to have a serious talk."

I said to TJ, "That goes for you, too."

The boys looked at each other, confused.

Dario had arrived, out of breath, in time to hear most of the recap. "I never believed Dr. Rodney was stalking Meredith," he said. "It was just a crazed fan."

Tucker looked up at the two girls in the cart at the top of the coaster. We all saw what he was seeing. Cassandra started to stand up.

"I have a bad feeling about this," I said.

"Way bad," Josie agreed.

"What should we do?" Timmy asked.

Then a voice from out of nowhere said, "I have an idea."

It was Apple, and she was standing next to me. Like *right* next to me, and I swear she hadn't been there a hot sec before.

"I wish you wouldn't do that. Seriously. I hate it—"

"Not now, Stell," said Dario. "What's your idea?" he asked Apple.

Surprisingly, she got to the point. "We should prepare for the worst." She pointed to the fat mat under the bungee.

"Good idea," Josie said. "Let's get it."

Tucker rolled his T-shirt sleeves up to his shoulders and flexed his biceps. "Sun's out, guns out. Let's do it."

The seven of us—me, Josie, the Three *T*s, Dario, and the Amazing Apple—went to the big mat. The boys pushed it, while we girls pulled.

"Ugh, this is heavy! Isn't it just full of air? Since when is air so heavy?" I said to Josie, "I'll start working out tomorrow."

"Where are Meredith's security guards?" Josie asked.

"Probably stuck in the fun house."

"Can't you do a trick or something to make this easier?" Josie asked Apple.

"Not a trick," she said. "But something."

Apple formed a loop with her thumb and index finger, put it into her mouth, and whistled to Lucien, Evan, and Austin, who were at the end of the pier, watching from the concert stage. They rushed over to provide the extra muscle we needed, and the mat moved to under the Minotaur, but it didn't cover all the possible angles someone could fall from.

I shielded my eyes from the sun and looked up to see Cassandra getting herself into position next to Meredith and holding her phone up for a selfie.

That's when everything started going in slow motion:

Meredith knocked the phone out of Cassandra's hand.

Cassandra leaned to get it.

She lost her balance.

And she began to fall.

I called to the boys, "She's coming down! To the right!"

We scrambled to get the mat to where Cassandra was headed. Her loud scream filled the air, mixed with the caws of seagulls and everyone else shouting and yelling.

After what seemed like forever, but was only a few seconds, Cassandra landed . . . mostly on the mat.

Fifty-Five

Stella

Murphy's Pier

June 25 (Continued)

We stood around Cassandra until an ambulance drove right out onto the pier. Paramedics secured her to a backboard, loaded her into the rig, and sped off with red and blue lights flashing.

Things slowed down after that.

The boys came around to our side of the bouncy mat. TJ rubbed his hand on my back. "It didn't look too bad. She'll be all right."

Timmy said, "I don't want to imagine what would've happened if we were a second slower."

Dario's cell phone alarm chirped. "I don't believe this, but I have to go to work," he said. "Of all times for a shift at the Gifty to start. I gotta run."

Josie said, "When duty calls . . . We'll text you later."

Booth directed the coaster operator to get it working and safely escorted Meredith off the ride. She was instantly surrounded by bodyguards and bandmates. They were within earshot, and I was eager to hear exactly what had happened up there.

"Are you okay?" Booth asked her.

She combed her fingers through her hair. "I'm fine."

"We have another ambulance on the way. They'll want to check you out."

"I said I'm fine."

Booth said, "I'd like a full account of what happened. Can you come down to the station for an interview?"

"That won't be necessary. I can tell you right here, right now."

Meredith looked over to us.

"She's going to thank us," Apple said.

Josie said to me, "She's going to tell him about the Smoothie Factory, the pier, and the jellies. This is the moment everything gets fixed."

"I think so," I said to both of them, and I stood up a little, proud of what we'd accomplished. It isn't every day you save a species and thousands of people.

Meredith pointed at us. "It was them!"

Booth looked over to us. Bodyguards looked at us. Even Evan, Austin, and Lucien stared at us.

"This is all their fault," she said. "Those girls kidnapped me."

"What?!" I said.

"Is she kidding?" Josie said.

Booth pointed to us and asked, "*Those* girls? Stella and Josie Higley?" He didn't believe what Meredith was saying.

"Yeah." She flipped her hair and smiled for incoming photos. "None of this would've happened if it hadn't been for them."

TJ whispered to me, "What did you two do?"

Tucker said, "Is this what you wanted to talk about? Were you going to flee the country or something?"

Tucker said, "Too late for that."

"It's not as bad as it sounds," I said.

Timmy said, "It sounds pretty bad."

"I think maybe it is," Josie said. "But not as bad as what you three were doing."

Apple said, "I'm outta here." And by the time I turned my head to thank her for helping us, she was gone.

Tucker asked, "Us? We didn't do anything."

"That you know of, which is part of the problem. You didn't even ask questions to know that what you were doing was harmful," Josie said. "Dreadfully harmful."

The Three *T*s looked at me for an answer.

"Your little eight p.m. rendezvous under the boardwalk," I hinted. "Did you stop to think for a hot sec about what you were actually doing?"

TJ began. "How do you—"

"That's not important," I said.

Meredith's security guard said to Booth, "Miss Maxwell needs to rest now. We can bring her to the station a little later to make an official statement. Why don't you deal with *those girls*, and we'll take care of her?"

Timmy said to us, "Look, the lady from the Smoothie Factory said it was fruit. The best, freshest fruit for her customers. She couldn't get it locally."

TJ defended him. "It's not like pineapples or coconuts grow in New Jersey."

Josie said, "Or wattle berries."

Timmy asked, "Wattle what?"

I said, "You were transporting their secret sauce. And that sauce has terrible side effects."

Tucker asked, "How were we supposed to know any of that? In fact, how do *you* know that?"

TJ said, "Seriously. It made sense that they needed fruit from the islands, and that it would be delivered by boat. So don't make us out to sound dumb."

Booth scratched his head and confirmed with Meredith one more time. "*Those* two girls kidnapped you? But you're right here."

Timmy said, "It's not like we kidnapped someone."

Meredith said to Booth, "Pay attention. They kidnapped me *before* I was right here."

"We didn't kidnap anyone!" I yelled.

"Tell me," Josie asked the boys. "What did they pay you to participate in their scheme?"

"Not a cent," Tucker said, then added, "Miss Smarty-Pants."

Booth nodded at Meredith Maxwell, then walked over to us. "Josie, Stella, what the heck happened?"

"You see—" I started.

"We can explain everything—" Josie added.

He held up his hand for us to stop talking. "We're gonna have to do this downtown after I get things sorted out here. That's gonna take me a little while. Then I'll drive you."

"Like, in a cop car?" I asked.

"In the back," he confirmed.

Fifty-Six

Stella

Police Station

June 26 (Continued)

"So there we were in the back seat of Officer Booth's squad car. He left the window cracked open, like you might for a dog. We could see and hear all the hub-bub."

"What I don't understand is that if you were in Booth's car, how come your dad brought you in here?" Santoro asks. "Why didn't you come in with Booth?"

"Can we just say that maybe all the choices we made yesterday weren't great?"

"I think that's an understatement," Santoro says. It's the type of comment that might be accompanied by a tension-breaking smile, but he doesn't crack his tough detective exterior. "What happened next?"

I explain. "Meredith was nearby on Thirty-Fourth Street with her security entourage. We watched her get checked out by an EMT and drink a bottle of water. Once a blood pressure cuff was removed, one of the thick-armed bodyguards said to Meredith, 'There's a radio news lady—duPluPlu. She wants to get a comment from you. Want me to tell her it's not a good time?' And Meredith said, 'I never refuse time with the media. Send her over. I have plenty to tell her.'"

Fifty-Seven

Stella

Thirty-Fourth Street
June 25 (Continued)

"*Now* she's gonna tell Murielle all about the Smoothie Factory."

Josie shushed me. They weren't far from us, but there was a lot of activity that made it hard to hear. "She's going to tell Murielle about the pier and the jellies. It's actually super smart of her to go to the media instead of Booth, because he probably won't believe it."

duPluie set a microphone in front of Meredith Maxwell. "I'm recording, so anytime you're ready."

Maxwell: I was in the fun house, just walking along enjoying seeing my reflection in those silly mirrors. You know the ones?

duPluie: I sure do.

Maxwell: Then I climbed over the rope bridge, and the next thing I knew, a girl pushed me through a hole in the floor, and I fell. I fell! To the sand below. Another girl closed the trapdoor, and the two of them kept me down there against my will. It was those Higley girls. They wouldn't let me leave.

duPluie: What did they want?

Maxwell: Ransom? Autographs? Who knows?

duPluie sucked in a shocking breath that would be audible on the recording.

"I'm going to go all New York on her," I said to Josie. "Watch me."

Then something amazing happened.

Fifty-Eight

Stella

Police Station

June 26 (Continued)

Detective Santoro asks, "Something amazing, huh? I could make a pretty good guess what that was."

"Yup. A voice, one we knew well, came out of nowhere. It said, 'She's lying, and it makes you wonder why, doesn't it?'"

"Apple. That boardwalk magician?" he asks.

I nod. "You know, she's more like a superhero. She seems to know when we need her, and she appears without so much as a Bat-Signal." I say, "She unlocked the door and let us— Wait. Is that a crime? If it is, then that's not what happened."

"Stella, believe me on this. Alayna Appleton opening a car door is small potatoes compared to everything else we got going

on here. So I promise you, she will not get in any trouble. But for future reference, don't do that again."

"Noted," I say. "So we left Booth's car. We were on a mission. To figure out why Meredith was lying." Then I added, "If we weren't going to find out, who would?"

Fifty-Nine

Stella

Nifty Gifty

June 25 (Continued)

Not sure exactly where to go for help, we slipped into the only safe place we could think of, Nifty Gifty.

"What the heck?" Dario asked when he saw us. "I heard everything on the radio news. Get back here." He dragged us behind the counter, pushed us to where no one could see, and tossed us each a big straw beach hat and sunglasses. "Put these on." He smiled at a customer. "Have you checked out those refrigerator magnets? A sight to behold, I promise you. They're right over there." Then to us he said, "I'm pretty sure I'm now implicated as an accomplice or something."

"Toughen up, Dario," I said to him. "We seriously need intel on why Meredith won't tell the police about the

Smoothie Factory and why she's lying about what we did to her."

"Way ahead of you, Higleys. Way, way ahead."

A customer approached the register. "These are excellent choices," Dario said to her about the magnets she'd chosen. Then he took her snow globe and wrapped it in tissue paper. "I always wonder what the fascination is with snow globes. I love them myself, but they freak me out a little too, because I imagine, *What if I was trapped inside?* Do you ever do that?"

"Not so much," the customer said.

"And here's your change. Have a wonderful day."

Once the customer was out of the way, I said to Dario, "Can we leave the snow globe commentary for another day, when our freedom isn't hanging in the balance?"

"Stella, don't be rude, because as I look around, I'm pretty much the only friend you guys have right now. Where are your Three *T*s, huh? So, if I were you, I'd try to be a little nicer to me."

"Fine," I growled.

"Fine what?" he asked.

"Snow globes are cool," I spat. "Now, what are you way ahead on?"

"Research, Stella, research. That's what a good radio journalist does. I've been looking into a variable that you girls forgot about. A biggie."

Josie asked, "What?"

"It's what makes the world go around. The lettuce, the cabbage, the dough—"

Josie said, "Stop with the food!"

"The money!" he said. "Meredith is lying because of *money*."

"How does any of this connect to money?" I asked.

And he showed us.

Sixty

Stella

Police Station
June 26 (Continued)

"What Dario found out was that the Smoothie Factory is funded by something called a shell company, which he explained isn't a real company but one that's only used for financial transactions. It's fake."

Santoro says, "I know what a shell company is. And," he adds, "I'm impressed that you do too."

"Gee, thanks, Detective. Can I call you Jay?"

Straight face: "No."

"Okay, well, thanks anyway. That's the only nice thing you've said to me all day."

He rubs his scruff. "Just continue."

"The shell company is called MM Enterprises, and guess

who holds the money for that company?" I don't wait for him to answer. "Miss I Hate the Environment, Miss I'm a Big Fat Liar, Miss I Don't Care If People Drown on a Pier, Miss I'm Gonna Blame All This on Stella and Josie Higley, Miss—"

"I get it," he says.

"If she tells the truth, the Smoothie Factory doesn't go national, and she loses all the money she's invested." I bang my hands on the table. "Bam!" I say. "Case closed. Open and shut! I rest my case. Thank you, jury, for your time."

Santoro puts his pen down and leans his head right and left to get a good stretch. It even cracks. He doesn't speak. It's the silence thing he's been doing all along.

This time, I don't fill it.

Santoro looks at his watch.

"Why isn't there a clock in here?" I ask.

"So the perps lose all sense of time."

"I'm not a perp."

"Should you be?"

"We didn't do anything wrong."

Santoro shakes his head.

"Okay, so a few things. But they were for the right reason, and they were—"

"I know, they were all your idea."

"Exactly." I say, "You know, you're a really good listener. You know that?"

He exhales loudly. "It's three o'clock in the morning. You can go hang out with your dad and sister. I'm gonna talk to some people."

"Pull strings?"

"Nope. I don't do that. I told your dad that, and I meant it."

Sixty-One

Stella

The Smoothie Factory
June 25 (Continued)

Dario said to us, "I think I know how to take care of this." He led us to the Nifty storeroom and moved boxes of snow globes for us to sit on. "Stay here." And he left us.

After a few seconds, he came back in and handed us an old-fashioned radio with a twisty knob. "You can listen on the radio." Then he added, "And for real, guys, I mean it—stay here."

> "Murielle duPluie here with continuing coverage of the Meredith Maxwell situation. The starlet is resuming her promo tour with her next stop at our very own hot spot for cool, healthy drinks, the Smoothie Factory, where the one and only

> Meredith Maxwell is mixing fruity concoctions for herself. Only security and press, like myself, are allowed inside the store. There's a sizable crowd outside the windows watching the rock star make her smoothie."

My cell phone rang with a video call. It was Dario. I turned the volume down on the radio as duPluie asked Meredith about the flavors she was blending, and I put my phone on speaker so Josie could hear too. Dario's face—well, more like his chin—appeared on the screen. "Okay. I'm going in."

"How will you get in?" Josie asked.

"I have a press badge."

"From where?" I asked.

"Duh, a printer."

"No one is going to believe that," I said. "You're thirteen."

He held it up for us to see. It wasn't too bad. "Maybe it'll work," I said to Josie.

There was commotion on Dario's end of the phone, and we could see bodies all around him. He said, "Excuse me. Press. Member of the press. Please move aside."

Then there was a deep voice, and we could see the profile of one of Meredith's thick-chested bodyguards. "Can I help you?"

"Uh, yeah, hi there. Dario Imani. Intern at Shelter

Harbor Public TV, Channel Nine. I was sent out here to get in on this press conference." He held up his badge for the guy.

Dario said, "It's my first interview, so kind of a big deal to my future as a journalist. I'm so nervous. Do you think she'll be able to tell? Do I look nervous?"

The guy handed the badge back and opened the door to the Smoothie Factory.

"Thanks, man. Hey, this is for you." Dario reached into his pocket and handed something to the guard. *A tip?*

The guard held the object up just high enough for us to catch a glimpse of a refrigerator magnet that said SHELTER HARBOR, NJ. Dario had thought of everything.

"Thanks, kid," the guard said. "Just relax. You'll be fine."

Then Dario whispered into the phone, "I'm in. My digital video recorder will stream through the phone, so you can see it all. Hanging up now."

A new image appeared on the phone. It was the Smoothie Factory from the perspective of Dario's handheld video recorder. Meredith Maxwell sat across from duPluie, and they were talking.

duPluie: So, Meredith, what's your favorite flavor?
Maxwell: I love pineapple with fresh coconut.
duPluie: Sounds like the tropics in a cup.

They noticed Dario getting closer.

Murielle duPluie pushed a button on her microphone and asked Dario, "Can I help you?"

"Hey there. Dario Imani. Intern at Shelter Harbor Public TV, Channel Nine." He held out his badge for them to see.

"Channel Nine?" duPluie asked. "I didn't know they had interns. Are you working for Lauri Witte?"

"No. For Sue Walsh. She sends her best."

DuPluie thought. "Sue? I don't think I know her."

"Well, she knows you. Admires you, actually, and she really wants me to get this story. She gave me some questions to ask. Do you mind?"

"I never mind TV filming me," Meredith said. "Fire away."

Murielle duPluie said, "We weren't quite done with this."

"We can come back to it," Meredith assured her, and flipped her hair.

Murielle spoke into a gadget on her wrist. "Alessandro, go to commercial." And duPluie made a motion with her hand as if to say, *Go on ahead, Mr. Big Shot Intern.*

"Great," Dario said. "My first question, Ms. Maxwell, is about your beauty regime. I mean, we can all see how beautiful and fit you are. What's your secret?"

Meredith smiled.

I asked Josie, "When did he become such a charmer?"

She said, "I don't know, but he's good."

Meredith said, "Oh, you're so kind. But my secret is right here. You're looking at it. These smoothies are the best thing for your health and your appearance. I can't get enough of them."

"And do you have financial ties to the Smoothie Factory? I mean, if this store goes national, how much money do you stand to make?"

"What? Why would you ask that?"

"Well, because according to my research, you're the president of a holding company called MM Enterprises that has provided the capital for this store, and MM—um, you—stand to make a load of money if it does well. How big is your financial stake in the company?"

Instantly Meredith looked annoyed but quickly covered it with a dazzling smile. She brushed her hair out of her face in one direction, then another. "I don't know what you're talking about."

Dario said, "Oh, my bad, sorry. We can move to some other questions, if that's better."

"I think it would be," Meredith said.

"Great. Are you aware that the Smoothie Factory is illegally bringing wattle berries from Australia to New Jersey, and that's the secret ingredient in the smoothie's stellar nutrition? And are you aware that the processing of those berries is happening right here in the basement? And that this processing creates a by-product that's drained into the ocean and kills medusa jellyfish as well as damages the pylons that support Murphy's Pier?"

Meredith asked, "Where are you getting this information?"

Dario kept right on going. "And now the pier can't support the weight of the people who'll attend your concert?"

"That is a crazy accusation," Meredith snapped, and she looked super nervous.

Dario didn't back down.

"So is that a yes or a no?"

Meredith paused.

Murielle duPluie clicked her microphone back on. "We're back on the air, folks, and Meredith Maxwell has just been slammed with a host of accusations about her financial ties to the Smoothie Factory, which she's promoting here today—a store, by the way, allegedly tied to environmentally reckless business practices."

Meredith looked into Dario's camera.

"Tell us, Meredith, what do you know about this?" asked duPluie.

Meredith's mouth couldn't form a single word. She waved to a girl on her team who was sitting on the sideline. The girl said to Murielle and Dario, "We're gonna have to cut this interview short, I'm afraid."

Dario asked the girl, "Can we schedule a follow-up?"

"You can leave me your business card, and I'll call you."

"Not so fast. The people of Whalehead deserve an answer," said duPluie.

Murielle pushed a button on her earpiece, listening to someone.

duPluie: I have Mayor Lopez on the line now. Hi there, Mayor. Thank you for taking our call.

Mayor: No problem, Murielle. I love the Smoothie Factory, and I'm happy to talk about how healthy I feel now that I've been having a smoothie every day.

duPluie: Are you aware, sir, that the ingredients in those smoothies are creating a dangerous situation in the ocean? One that's affecting the aquatic life, and could very well hurt our community?

Mayor: Uh, I'm not sure what you're talking about, Murielle.

Dario: Sure you are, Mr. Mayor. Because you've made promises to people in exchange for their help with this illegal activity.

duPluie: Mr. Mayor, what do you have to say?

There was the sound of a click.

"It seems we've lost the mayor. I'm sorry, folks, but you have my word that WLEO will follow this story."

Meredith's bodyguards were inside the store now, pushing Dario and Murielle duPluie out. Dario kept recording.

Once on the outside of the crowd, we could see Murielle duPluie on the video. She faced Dario squarely. "How did you know that stuff?"

"I would never reveal my sources."

"Good answer. What's Channel Nine paying you as an intern?"

"Uh . . ."

"I'll double it."

"Um. I, uh . . ."

"Fine. I'll triple it. You drive a hard bargain, kid. You work for me now. I want to see everything you got. Let's get out of this heat and back to my office. We've got a story to blow the lid off of."

Sixty-Two

Stella

Storeroom, Nifty Gifty

June 25 (Continued)

The storeroom door opened, and there stood Dad. "What the heck is going on?"

"How did you find us?" Josie asked.

Dad held up his cell phone and showed us our dots. "There's an app for that, you know?" Then he said, "Let's go."

"Dad, we can explain everything," I said.

"No time, Stell. I have a pal at the police station. He's a detective. You're gonna tell him everything."

"Everything?" I asked.

"Everything, Stella," he said. "It's all gonna be fine. Trust me on this."

Josie and I walked out of the stuffy storeroom.

"Girls—"

I expected something comforting. Something empathetic. Something helpful. "Yeah, Dad?"

"Those hats look ridiculous."

Sixty-Three

Stella

Police Station

June 26 (Continued)

There's a knock on the interview room door.

Santoro reaches his long arm over but can't quite reach the knob, so he gets up. I see Gregory on the other side.

"Morning, Counselor," Santoro says.

Gregory looks right at me. "How you doing, Stell?"

"Okay?" I say.

He nods and smiles at me. It's a don't-worry-about-anything smile. Then he says to Santoro, "Let's talk."

Santoro nods.

As he's leaving, Gregory tells me, "I told your mom not to worry, but call her, okay?"

"I will."

Sixty-Four

Stella

Police Station

June 26 (Continued)

Dad, me, and Josie are eating breakfast in the cafeteria when Santoro sits next to us with a cup of coffee. He says, "Sorry that took so long. You can go."

"Thanks, Jay," Dad says.

Gregory walks up behind Santoro. The two shake hands. "Ready?" Gregory asks us.

We're so ready.

"You girls were very helpful to the police tonight," Gregory says as he holds the police station door open for us. "I heard everything. Santoro let me listen through the interview room speakers on my drive here. And I was on the phone with both of your moms all night."

Overhead an airplane dragging an advertisement for Moe's Raw Bar and Karaoke flies by.

"You were?" I ask.

"Of course, kiddo. We were all watching out for you."

"Thanks, Gregory," I say, and I hug him around the waist, because he's so much taller than me. Suddenly his name doesn't sound so stupid.

"You can always count on me," he says, and he ruffles my hair. It's goofy, but I like it. Maybe the change that came when Gregory married Mom hasn't been all bad.

Just then Laney pulls up in Dad's truck. "Need a lift?" She slides over and lets Dad drive.

Gregory opens the door for us, and Josie hops in. "Enjoy the rest of your summer," he calls in to her. To me he says, "I convinced your mom that this isn't a strike, but please stay out of trouble, Stell."

"I will."

"See you, Gary," Gregory says to my dad.

"Sure. Thanks again."

"Anytime."

Gregory walks away, and I'm about to get in after Josie when a voice calls to us, "Wait. Can I grab a ride?" It's Dr. Rodney.

"Of course," Dad says, and Dr. Rodney slides into the back seat between me and Josie.

I hear Murielle duPluie on the radio. "Dad," I say, "turn it up."

> "Murielle duPluie here with the Whalehead news from the Jersey Shore. I'm in front of the police station, where Stella and Josie Higley are exiting the building with their father and lawyer.
>
> "Oh, this is surprising. Dr. Rodney Klinger is also leaving the building and joining the Higleys in their car. And here comes Detective Jay Santoro.
>
> "Detective, Murielle duPluie from WLEO. Can you tell me what's going on?"

Dad drives the pickup out of the parking lot slowly as we all listen.

> "Here is what I can tell you, Ms. duPluie. First and foremost, the safety of the members of this community and our visitors is our highest priority. While the investigation is ongoing, I can confirm that the victim in this case, Cassandra Winterhalter, also known as Meredith Maxwell's number one fan, is now in stable condition. The suspect who was being questioned for stalking

Meredith Maxwell has been released, as those allegations were completely without merit."

Dr. Rodney asks, "What I want to know is, did *everyone* think I was some major Meredith Maxwell fan?"

"You might not know this," I say, "but you have sort of a vibe that some people might not totally be able to read—"

"Shh," Laney interrupts. "There's more." She turns the volume up.

Santoro continues. "In addition, we have issued three arrest warrants, one for Mayor Paul Lopez for endangering the welfare of this community and its visitors, and a second for Mrs. Gabriella Gardiner for illegally dumping toxic substances into the ocean. The third is for the pop star Meredith Maxwell for insider trading."

We pass Booth driving his police cruiser, with Meredith Maxwell in the back.

duPluie: What about Meredith Maxwell's allegations that Stella and Josephine Higley kidnapped her?

Santoro: No charges are being filed with regard to any alleged kidnapping. I cannot comment further as there are elements of this that are ongoing.

duPluie: Can you tell us the future of the Smoothie Factory?

Santoro: I have to get back into the precinct, but I understand that the Flying Fish are issuing an announcement shortly. I think your listeners will find that interesting.

duPluie: Thanks for the tip. WLEO listeners, please let me introduce my new intern, Dario Imani, who is on location at Karleigh Park with the Flying Fish rock-and-roll band. Over to you, Dario.

Josie and I clap with excitement about Dario's new internship.

Dr. Rodney reaches a hand to each of us and gently stops our applause so that we can hear.

Imani: Dario Imani here with WLEO News, reporting live from Karleigh Park, where Evan Roberts, lead guitarist of the Flying Fish, is walking to a podium. The next voice you hear will be the great Evan Roberts.

Roberts: Thank you for joining me. There's only one thing performers hate more than disappointing their fans, and that's finding out that one of their trusted bandmates is poisoning the ocean in the name of profit. For this reason, Austin, Lucien,

> and myself have chosen to cut all ties with Meredith Maxwell and dissolve the Flying Fish.

There are sounds of groans from the crowd, and also in the car.

> Evan Roberts: "While that is certainly sad news for you to hear, we hope you'll be pleased to know that me and the guys are forming a new group, Sea Vacuum. And this is more than a music group. It's also an ingenious invention that sucks oil and pollution out of the ocean. It was invented by a local scientist named Dr. Rodney Klinger."

We all look at Dr. Rodney. Dr. Rodney holds his hands up. "What can I say? I'm a scientific genius. Maybe that's the vibe some people aren't able to read. And, mark my words, the sea vacuum has the potential to transform our oceans." Then he says, "I've been talking to Roberts about this for a while. I'm friends with his dad."

> Evan Roberts: "The mission of our new band is not only to bring our fans the best music, but also to raise awareness of the need for ocean cleanup. To launch our new band, we'll be hosting a free concert right here in Karleigh Park. We hope everyone can make it.

"To give you a taste of what to expect, the boys and I are gonna play a quick song for you. . . . Two, three, four!"

And the car fills with rock music as Evan belts out the new song.

Dr. Rodney jams on air drums, me and Josie on air guitar, Laney on air keyboard. Dad bops his head up and down to the beat.

Our jam is cut short with a chime from Laney's phone.

She takes the call:

"Yes, sir. . . . I see. . . . I'm on my way."

Dad asks, "What was that about?"

"Is there any way you can take me to Finnegan's Marina? I have a little thing to do for work."

"Sure," Dad says. "When you said you worked for the Coast Guard, I didn't realize it was an on-call-type thing."

"Only sometimes. But I can't talk about that."

"Why not?" Josie asks.

"Top secret?" I ask.

"What are you? A spy?" Dad laughs at his own joke.

Dr. Rodney says, "It's classified, isn't it?"

She nods.

Dad slows down at the marina. "Like, *classified* classified?"

Laney says, "Yup. Sorry, guys. Confidential. I really can't talk about it."

Part Four

Josie

Sixty-Five

Finnegan's Marina—Whalehead, New Jersey

June 26 (Continued)

"You can let me out here," Laney says.

Dad stops the pickup truck, and Laney slides out.

She says to all of us, "See you tonight for the next round of Monopoly. Get the board set up. I'll be there."

We watch her walk away, and Dad puts the truck in reverse, but Stella says, "Wait. Let's watch."

Dad puts the truck back in park.

A Coast Guard tugboat pushes a boat to the dock.

"The *Koala,*" Stella says.

Laney turns her reversible zip hoodie inside out, revealing SPECIAL AGENT on the back.

"She's a secret agent," Stella says. "I knew something was up with her!"

"Now, that's cool," Dr. Rodney says. "I have lots and lots to talk to her about."

She leads a man off the boat in handcuffs. It's the man from the pictures on her phone. Other agents board the boat and leave with bags.

"Wattle berries," I say.

"Just like you told Santoro," Dad says.

Dr. Rodney says, "I didn't know what was damaging the pier or hurting the medusas, but you girls figured it out."

A police cruiser with lights and sirens blaring schreeches to a stop in front of the marina. Laney leads the handcuffed guy to the car.

Detective Santoro gets out and opens the back door for the Australian wattle berry smuggler. He exchanges words with Laney, and the two share a fist bump.

I truly can't believe what happens next. Detective Santoro looks over to our truck, he waves to Dad and us, and then, finally, the man cracks a smile.

Sixty-Six

Josie

Beach

June 27

"Good morning, Whalehead. It's Dario Imani here from the Jersey Shore. Turns out that the Sea Vacuum music group likes our little town and plans to set down some roots. This is evident by the fact that today they bought the former Smoothie Factory building. A statement from the group reports that it will reopen as a Water Ice Factory with a rock-and-roll theme. A portion of all profits will be donated to marine conservation. I never liked those smoothies anyway.

"Gonna be a hot one today, WLEO listeners, so stay cool."

Stella and I hop onto the hot sand to find a spot to lie out. We don't get too far before a four-wheeler pulls along-side us. Timmy drives, and TJ drops a rescue board onto the ground for us to stand on.

I say, "Thanks so much. The sand is wicked hot today."

"Where's your third wheel?" Stella asks about Tucker.

"Running, if you can believe that," TJ says. "He actually has to pass the fitness test in a few days."

Timmy says, "In fact, here he comes now."

Tucker looks like he's rolled in the sand with sweaty skin. He's bright red and panting. "I remember why I hate running."

"Why?" Timmy asks.

"Because, um, running is the worst," Tucker says. "Hop off that thing. I'm riding back to the shack."

Timmy and TJ get off the four-wheeler to let their near-dead friend use it. I notice when they step onto the sand that they're wearing five-toed water shoes, so their feet are protected from the heat.

"Where are you guys setting up beach camp?" Timmy asks.

"Near the water," I say. I use very few words because I'm not sure what things are like between us since we accused them of helping the Smoothie Factory.

TJ turns his back to Stella. "Hop up. I'll get you there." She jumps onto his back. He bends down to grab the board and jogs toward a spot near the water. Then Timmy does the same for me.

Maybe Stella's idea of hanging out with lifeguards isn't so bad after all.

TJ puts Stella down in the water. She tosses her bag onto the dry sand, pulls off her cover-up, and throws it on top of the bag. Then she and TJ walk down the beach.

Timmy sets me down, and I spread my towel. He sits next to me. "Your feet okay?"

"Better. But now that I'm farther away from the boardwalk, not sure how I'll get home."

"I'm sure I can help a pretty girl with that."

"Pretty?" I ask.

"Yeah. I've been trying to tell you that all week, but you keep blowing me off."

"You have?"

"Uh, yeah. What do you have against lifeguards?" he asks.

"Nothing. I'm sorry I made you feel that way. I think you have a noble job, saving people from drowning and all."

"You forgot the part about wrestling sharks." He smiles, and, for the first time, I notice his dimples. *Have they always been there?* I look down the shoreline at the waves crashing, kids building castles, couples walking hand in hand, teens playing Frisbee, and vacationers soaking up the sun.

"And saving girls unprepared for hot sand." I add to the list of noble things about his job.

"Glad to help," he says.

There are a few beats of silence. "Hey, about the Smoothie

Factory, and the *Koala*, and kayaks, and everything. We didn't put it all together. We were just being dumb about the mayor's promise that we could skip a year in the training program. We didn't look at the whole picture."

"I know that," I say. "I'm sorry I yelled at you. Lopez is a bad guy. He lied to you, made promises you couldn't turn down. Gardiner did it to Angie, too. Promised her an awesome job in exchange for towing kayaks for you to use."

He nods.

"They'll get theirs. You know, I've been imagining the best punishments for them. I hope some judge sentences them to a life of scooping plastic out of the ocean. That would be better than just locking them up in jail."

"I like the way you think," he says. Then he surprises me and out of the blue says, "Thank you."

"For what?"

"You must've never mentioned us to the police. We weren't questioned or anything. The only way that could've happened was if you and Stella never told that detective what we were doing." He says, "You knew and you didn't tell."

I shrug.

"Are you going to the Sea Vacuum concert tonight?" he asks.

"Of course."

"Want to go together?" he asks. "My treat."

"It's free."

He bumps me with his shoulder. "I know."

"Okay. That sounds like ripper fun."

"Then it's a date," he says. And just like that, I have a date with a lifeguard (in training).

Sixty-Seven

Josie

Beach

June 27 (Continued)

Stella spreads her towel out next to me and flops down on her belly. "It's lumpy."

"What?"

"The sand."

"It's never as comfortable as it looks like it's gonna be. So," I say to Stella, and I tell her about Timmy and the concert.

"That's great. You like him?"

I say, "I really think I do."

Stella says, "Now that you've saved the ocean, and all those concertgoers, you can have some fun."

"I wish I could save the whole ocean," I say. "That's more than a one-woman job." I close my eyes. "How about you? And TJ?"

Stella says, "I like him for sure, but I'm not getting too attached. You know, just having fun hanging out with him this summer."

"Good plan." I block the sun from my eyes as I look at Stella. "I don't want to bring Peter up, but I was wondering something."

"What?"

"Why did you get in trouble for the doctored photos on social media?"

"Because I told the principal it was my idea."

"Why would you do that?"

"Because I knew about it and I didn't stop those girls and I should have. I thought being punished for it would make me feel better and also give me a good excuse to not hang around them anymore." Then Stella asks me, "Would you take the blame for something you didn't do?"

"To protect someone that I cared about, I would," I say, and then I see a whole new Dario coming down the beach. I sit up.

"What up, girls?" He turns his WLEO baseball hat around frontward and takes off his aviator sunglasses.

"You have a new look?" I ask.

He turns to show us his WLEO shirt—logo in the front,

REPORTER written across the back. "Well, I'm kind of a celebrity now, so I need to play the part, you know?"

"Oh, for sure," Stella says.

He sits in the sand between us, kicking some onto both of us when he does.

We groan a little and dust the sand off.

"So," Dario asks. "I gotta know, off the record, whose idea was it to kidnap Meredith Maxwell?"

Together, Stella and I point to each other and say, "It was her."

Sixty-Eight

Josie

Beach

June 27 (Continued)

Dr. Rodney gets us all—me, Stella, Timmy, TJ, Dad, Laney, and Tucker, who also invited former Smoothie Factory employee Lydia—special passes to the Sea Vacuum concert, right up front so we can see Evan, Austin, and Lucien.

Dario's at the side of the stage with a press pass and Apple. I'm not sure if he invited her as his guest, or if she just appeared.

The band rocks Karleigh Park, which is jam-packed with fans.

As we walk home from the park, I ask Dr. Rodney, "So, what happened in '02?"

He says, "Ah, the summer of the terrestrial beach landing.

That was the incident that proved flying saucers are flat and space beings are green."

"For real?"

"Actually, no, officially none of that ever happened, and I made it all up."

"Bummer. Unofficially?"

"I have the photos in the bungalow. Mark my words, it was as real as real can get. But"—he puts a finger in front of his mouth—"I signed something."

I zip my lip, and when my hand swings down, it finds Timmy's waiting to catch it. He asks, "Soft serve?"

Part Five

Stella

Sixty-Nine

Stella

Beach
June 28

"Dario Imani here with the Whalehead news from the Jersey Shore. The Sea Vacuum concert was a huge success, resulting in thousands of downloads of the band's newest hit.

"Vacationers should be aware that Murphy's Pier will be closed until the work crew has certified the stability of the pylons.

"In other news, Cassandra Winterhalter was discharged from Whalehead Hospital today."

Josie and I race down the boardwalk, weaving between weekenders soaking in the last minutes of sun and fun before returning to work tomorrow morning.

We pass our favorite shops, arcades, pizza places, and the old Smoothie Factory with a sign in the window: CLOSED.

We're just about to dash into Kevin's Fun House when Dr. Rodney stops us. "Whoa. Where's the fire?"

"Not a fire," I say. "Just something we need to take care of."

"I wanted to give this to you girls." He reaches into a canvas tote bag that's over his shoulder and pulls out our box . . . the original one.

"What?" I ask.

"Where did you get that?" Josie asks. "Have you had that all this time?"

He hands it to Josie. "Yeah, sorry. I always knew that you girls were up to something down there, and when the Smoothie Factory did all of their renovations, I thought I'd grab it and keep it safe. But then there was the toxin, the pier, Meredith Maxwell . . . well, you know. I just forgot about it. I'm really sorry."

Josie opens it and peeks inside. "It's all here," she says to me. "All our memories." Then she says to Dr. Rodney, "Thanks for looking after it."

"No problem."

I ask him, "So, what are you up to today?"

He secures his tote over his shoulder again and brushes crispy blond hairs out of his face. "There's a little matter of China, and importing and exporting, and a meeting with the government. And waves."

Gibberish as always with Dr. Rodney.

"Well, good luck with that. I can't wait to hear all about it," Josie says.

He holds a hand to his ear and says, "She's calling me, girls." He points to the water, which I assume is the "she," walks down the ramp, and drops the tote. Then he stops to talk to a girl. She's the girl from the pictures in his bungalow. "Hey, Dad!" She hugs him. His daughter.

We bypass the line.

I lead the way through the mirrors, where Josie stops to admire her extra-tall self. This time I do too. We quickly navigate the foam pillars and scale the bridge.

Josie looks right, then left. "No one's coming."

With the all clear, I stomp on one end of the floorboards, just like I did when Meredith was here.

We hop to the sand below, and I pull the trapdoor shut behind me.

"Josie," I say. "You covered for me, didn't you?"

"With Santoro?"

"Yeah. You said everything was your idea?"

"You can't get in trouble, Stella."

"Neither can you. What if that ruined your chances for the presidency?" I ask.

She shrugs. "I figured it was a low risk that the news would get back home."

"Well, thanks."

"You're my sister. I've always got your back," Josie says.

"And I've always got yours," I say.

"I know." After a hot sec Josie hunches over and walks to the tuft of grass where we hid the new box. She digs it up and transfers its contents to our old box.

Then she holds up a sticker from the Sea Vacuum concert. "My favorite day of the summer so far."

I hold up a strip of pictures from the photo booth at the arcade—me, Josie, and Dario, with Apple photobombing.

Josie scrambles the combination lock and sets the box back into the hole in the sand.

"This is the perfect summer," I say.

Josie says, "I hope nothing changes."

But like all perfect things . . .

Two Weeks Later

Josie

Seventy

Josie

Police Station

July 4

I sit in the interview room at the Whalehead police station. Again. I'm embarrassed to say that it's only been, like, two weeks since Dad brought us here to talk to his friend, the grouchy Detective Santoro. This time I'm a mess: My hair, skin, and clothes are still recovering after washing off wet cement—it's not a pretty sight.

"I just want to make clear that this was all my fault," I say.

Detective Santoro sighs and slides me a Coke. "But, things did change, didn't they, Josie?" he asks.

Acknowledgments

Like a day at the beach, writing is more fun with friends. Thanks to my amazing writing partners KB, Kathleen, Jane, June, Janis, Greg, John, and Ramona for their endless support and wisdom.

Special thanks to Lucien, Austin, and Evan for agreeing to be Sea Vacuum, and to Jay and Ian for playing the roles of good cop/bad cop.

If I could pick two people to share a secret hiding place under the boardwalk with, it would be my wonderful literary agent, Alyssa Henkin from Trident Media, and my editor, Alyson Heller. Thanks to you both for your continued council!

Of course, I'd never want to play Skee-Ball without my loves: Kevin, Ellie, Evan, and Happy.

Most of all, thank you to my readers, librarians, teachers, and parents who read and recommend my books. I hope you love *Saltwater Secrets* as much as the Lost In books, the Just Add Magic books, and *Sydney Mackenzie Knocks 'Em Dead.*

About the Author

Award-winning author Cindy Callaghan writes stuff tweens love to read. Her books—*Just Add Magic, Lost in London, Lost in Ireland* (previously titled *Lucky Me*), *Lost in Paris, Lost in Rome, Lost in Hollywood,* the award-winning *Sydney MacKenzie Knocks 'Em Dead, Potion Problems,* and *Saltwater Secrets*—magically capture the tween voice and experience.

Cindy's first book, the much-loved *Just Add Magic,* is now a breakout Amazon Original live-action series.

When asked what it is about her books that tweens love, she chuckles and says, "The funny! Without a doubt, it's the funny situations, characters, and dialogue."

In addition to writing, Cindy's passions include animal advocacy, running, moviegoing, reading, podcasts, wine, and girlfriends, all of which take a back seat to her three children, husband, and menagerie of rescued pets.

Cindy holds an MA and an MBA. The Delawarean (by way of Los Angeles) is a Jersey girl at heart. She lives in Wilmington and escapes to her Pennsylvania mountain retreat whenever time will allow.